'Who is *she*?' he questioned, standing transfixed in the doorway.

'She's my daughter,' Tessa told him. 'Her name is Poppy.'

'How old is she?' he asked hoarsely.

'Three.'

'Is she mine too?' he questioned after a pause, in barely a whisper as the colour drained from his face.

She shook her head and watched the dark hazel of his eyes become veiled.

'Who *is* her father then?' he choked as the small vision on the bottom step rubbed her eyes sleepily.

'Poppy is my adopted daughter,' she told him. 'Her parents were killed in a car crash and we got to know each other when she was brought into Horizons with a bleed behind her eyes from the accident. She was with us for quite some time and we became close. I used to sit beside her whenever I got a spare moment and take her a little surprise every day. In the end I applied to adopt her and was successful. So there you have it. No cause for alarm.'

Turning, she scooped Poppy up into her arms and held her close.

As their glances met she told him, 'Poppy has brought joy into my life.'

'Yes, I'm sure that she must have,' he said.

Dear Reader,

Hello once again. In this book, *A Father for Poppy*, I have left Heatherdale for a while and chosen another delightful place to set this story—namely, The Cotswolds, where in a famous eye hospital two people who have lost contact meet up again and make up for lost time as they find a deeper meaning to their relationship.

I hope that you will enjoy getting to know Drake and Tessa, with romance in the air once more.

Do you believe, as I do, that love makes the world go round?

Abigail Gordon
(From Marple Bridge, where the river bends…)

A FATHER
FOR POPPY

BY
ABIGAIL GORDON

First published in Great Britain 2015
by Mills & Boon, an imprint of Harlequin (UK) Limited,
Eton House, 18-24 Paradise Road, Richmond, Surrey, TW9 1SR

© 2015 Abigail Gordon

ISBN: 978-0-263-25941-4

Harlequin (UK) Limited's policy is to use papers that are natural,
renewable and recyclable products and made from wood grown in
sustainable forests. The logging and manufacturing processes conform
to the legal environmental regulations of the country of origin.

Printed and bound in Great Britain
by CPI Antony Rowe, Chippenham, Wiltshire

Abigail Gordon loves to write about the fascinating combination of medicine and romance from her home in a Cheshire village. She is active in local affairs, and is even called upon to write the script for the annual village pantomime! Her eldest son is a hospital manager, and helps with all her medical research. As part of a close-knit family, she treasures having two of her sons living close by, and the third one not too far away. This also gives her the added pleasure of being able to watch her delightful grandchildren growing up.

Books by Abigail Gordon

Heatherdale's Shy Nurse
Christmas Magic in Heatherdale
Swallowbrook's Wedding of the Year
Marriage Miracle in Swallowbrook
Spring Proposal in Swallowbrook
Swallowbrook's Winter Bride
Summer Seaside Wedding

**Visit the author profile page
at millsandboon.co.uk for more titles**

For my dear friend Jill Jones.

CHAPTER ONE

THEY HAD MADE love for the last time with the evening sun laying strands of gold across them. It had been as good as it had always been—sweet, wild and passionate. But there had been sadness inside Tessa because deep down she'd known it was the end of the affair, although neither of them were prepared to put into words that it was over.

It had been the agreement when they'd met— no commitments, take what life offered and enjoy it. Wedding rings were a joke, brushed to one side with babies and mortgages. Having spent her young years amongst her parents' quarrelling, unfaithfulness and eventual divorce, she was wary of the kind of hurts that a gold band on the finger could bring.

So she'd kept her distance from the men she'd met until Drake Melford had appeared in her life and everything had changed. He hadn't asked anything of her except to make love and when they had it had been magical. There had been no suggestion of any kind of commitment and in the beginning she'd been totally happy.

The attraction between them had been intense. So much so that when they'd been together at either of their apartments they'd made love on the rug, the kitchen table, and even once on a park bench in moonlight when the place had been empty, giving no thought to the future. Only the present had mattered.

So what had gone wrong? Something had changed the magic into doubt and misgivings, telling her in lots of ways that it was over, and whenever she'd wanted to ask Drake what was happening to them there had been the 'no strings' pact that had made the words stick in her throat.

Her only comfort had been in knowing that she wasn't competing against another woman, that it was his career that was going to take him away from her, and ever since then Tessa had kept the memory of that time buried deep in one of the past chapters of her life.

But a fleeting glimpse of the back of a man's neck and the dark thatch of hair above it as he'd got into a taxi outside a London railway station had been a reminder that anything as memorable as the time she'd spent with Drake Melford would never stay buried.

She brushed a hand across her eyes as if to shut out a blinding light. It wasn't the first time she'd given in to wishful thinking, and she knew how hard she had to fight to keep sane once the raw and painful memories were allowed to intrude into the life she had worked so hard to build in Drake's absence.

She groaned softly and an old lady next to her in the taxi queue asked, 'Are you all right, dear?'

Managing a smile, Tessa told her that it was just a stitch in her side instead of a thorn in her heart.

It was a Friday. She was in London for an important meeting and at the moment of seeing the man at the front of the queue getting into the taxi her thoughts were on what lay ahead and any surprise announcements that might be made.

She'd travelled up from Gloucestershire, where she was employed for the yearly AGM that was held in the city, and intended on staying the night at a hotel and catching an early train back in the morning.

Horizons Eye Hospital was on the edge of the elegant town of Glenminster, with the green hills of the county looking down on it, and was renowned for its excellence in specialised treatment. Tessa was employed there in a senior management position and was deeply committed to every aspect of it.

She'd heard it said that the health service had more managers than doctors. Though she, of course, respected the fantastic work done by the medical teams, at least a doctor didn't have to get up in the middle of the night when a patient who had arrived with valuables in their possession and asked that they be put in the hospital safe was unexpectedly being discharged and wanted their belongings returned to them. As the only key holder, this meant a deal of trouble for Tess.

It had also been said that she must wish that her position there was more connected with healing than organising. But Tess had always believed that a clean, healthy and efficient facility with good, wholesome food did as much for a patient's recovery as the medical miracles performed there.

As her taxi pulled up outside the building where the meeting was to take place, she was remembering a veiled comment that the chairman of the hospital board had made to her.

The top consultant of the hospital was retiring, so would be saying his goodbyes at the AGM, and the chairman had remarked that, much as the hospital was already famous, the man who was to replace him was going to take it even higher on the scale of excellent ophthalmology. When she'd asked for a name he'd just smiled and said, 'All will be revealed at the AGM.'

And now here she was, still too bogged down with the past to be curious about the present, until she walked into the conference room and realised that this time she hadn't been wrong in thinking she'd seen him. Drake Melford was there, chatting to some of her colleagues in his usual relaxed manner. It was history repeating itself.

Tessa turned quickly and made her way to a powder room, where a face devoid of colour stared back at her from the mirror. She closed her eyes, trying to shut out what she'd seen out there, telling herself that she should have known it was Drake that she'd glimpsed at the taxi rank.

She'd caressed his neck countless times, pressing kisses on to the strong column of it, raking her fingers through the dark pelt of his hair... But the meeting was due to start any moment and the chairman would not be expecting her to be skulking in the powder room.

The hospital board was already seated around a big oval table when she went back into the room, with Drake, the chairman and the retiring consultant seated centrally. When he saw her, Drake felt his heartbeat quicken and wished that their meeting—after what felt like a lifetime of regret—had been a more private one. But a part of him knew it was better this way, as a casual meeting of old friends, rather than... Rather than what? he asked himself.

As she eased herself into a seat at the far end of the table, Tessa listened to what was being said as if it were coming from another planet.

The chairman was making a presentation to the retiring consultant, who was following it with a short farewell speech, and then Drake would be introduced to those who would be working with him at the famous hospital.

He received a warm welcome from the chairman, who described him as a local man, top of his field in ophthalmology, and who, having fulfilled his obligation to a Swiss clinic, had agreed to accept the position of chief consultant at the Horizons Hospital.

There was loud applause. Tessa joined in weakly. Then Drake was on his feet, speaking briefly about the pleasure of being back in the U.K. and how he was looking forward to being amongst them. For

Tessa it was like a dream from which she was sure she would awaken at any moment.

After that, routine matters were discussed and soon the assembled members retired to a nearby hotel where an evening meal had been arranged for all those present.

So far the two of them hadn't spoken, but when she was chatting to one of the members of the hospital board, Drake went past with some of the bigwigs and called across, 'Hi, Tessa. You're still around, I see.'

She made no reply, just smiled a tight smile at the thought of being referred to as part of the fixtures and fittings. It was hardly the reunion her fevered brain had imagined during all those nights of tossing and turning.

As the evening wore on it seemed that quite a few of those at the meeting were booked in at the hotel for the night, Drake amongst them. Every time she thought of him being under the same roof she had to pinch herself to believe it.

Leaving most of them settled in the bar after they'd eaten, she went to her room and tried to come to terms with the day's events. The first time she'd met him had been mesmerising and today had been no different, though for a different reason, she thought, lying wide-eyed against the pillows.

The most mind-blowing thought was that after three years of being denied his presence, she would now be seeing him on a daily basis. How was she going to cope with that? Their agreement had made it easy for him to leave her when the opportunity for a promotion had landed at his feet, and there had been no word of any kind from him since he'd left. Not one. And now they would be colleagues again. Tessa groaned into her pillow.

Drake had gone to his hotel room shortly after her and there was no smile on his face now. When he'd received the offer to work in Switzerland everything else had faded into the background. It had been a chance to improve his expertise and he'd been so keen to get over there he had given no thought to what he and Tessa had shared, so obsessed had he been with his own affairs.

It had only been as the months had become years without her that he'd realised what he'd lost in his arrogance. Too much time had passed for him to get in touch with her again, and he had felt...what? Regret? Shame?

For all he knew, she might be married with a couple of little ones, he'd told himself whenever the desire to be with her had surfaced. He'd hoped it wouldn't stop him from making amends if the opportunity ever presented itself, and almost as if the fates had read his mind had come news of the vacancy at Horizons Hospital. Discovering that Tessa was now a senior manager at the hospital was only an additional bonus, he told himself.

He'd been anticipating her arrival at the meeting and observed the dismay in her expression when she'd seen him. There would be no warm welcome or happy reunion.

Then, fool that he was, he had made it a certainty by the patronising manner in which he'd greeted her when the meeting was over, as if she had been stagnating while he'd been on top of the world. Some of the Swiss Alps had actually seemed like the top of the world, but he'd had no chance to explore them because he'd always been too busy fulfilling his contract. He could no longer deny that he had been hoping for a different homecoming, and was plagued by flashes of memory of how things had once been between them.

In her room just down the corridor Tessa was also remembering when she and Drake had first met. It had been at a hospital staff meeting when he'd come to talk about some advances he had made in his work.

She'd arrived not intending staying long as her job was in Administration, but had been curious to see the man who was making a name for himself in eye surgery.

He'd been chatting laughingly to a group of nurses who'd been hanging on his every word as they'd waited for the meeting to begin, and Tess had been struck by dark good looks.

Having seen her arrive, he'd stepped to one side to get a better look and from the way his glance had kindled she'd known that he'd liked what he'd been seeing. Slim, elegant, with hair the colour of ripe corn, and wearing a black suit with a white silk top, Tessa Gilroy had been used to the appraisal of the opposite sex, but had rarely allowed it to proceed further than that. Her job had taken up most of her time and she'd accepted that.

But the stranger, tall and straight-backed with eyes of warm hazel and a thick, dark pelt of hair, had seemed different from any man she'd ever met, and when he'd been introduced to her as Drake Melford she'd known why.

His name had been mentioned frequently in medical circles because he'd been new, different, with a vivid, unorthodox approach that had got results, and she was to find that his attitude towards her would be the same.

Their only contact on that occasion had been a brief handshake on being introduced, and when the meeting had ended she'd left, leaving him encircled once again by admiring medical folk.

Her doorbell had rung at six the next morning and she'd found Drake Melford on the step. 'I couldn't sleep for thinking about you,' he said. 'Can I come in?'

Barefooted in a white cotton nightdress, she nodded and stepped back to let him pass, as if welcoming a man she barely knew into her apartment at that hour was something she did all the time.

She made a breakfast of sorts and they ate without speaking, eyes locked over every mouthful of food, and halfway through he pushed his chair back, lifted her up into his arms and carried her into the bedroom.

The first time they made love was rapturous. She was so in tune with his desires and the magic of his presence that it felt as if she had been waiting all her life for him to appear in it.

For the rest of the time it was slower and more sensual, and when at last Drake lay on top of the silk coverlet with his arms behind his head, he said with a slow smile on his face, 'Wow! I haven't felt like this in years, Tessa. You are incredible.'

It was then that they made the pact, still drowsy with fulfilment but not so sated that they couldn't think straight.

They would take it as it came, they agreed. No ties, no commitments, no promises. There would be no babies or mortgages.... An open-ended affair.

And when Drake got dressed after that last time and slung his things into a couple of suitcases Tessa watched him in mute misery, eyes shadowed, mouth unsmiling. She didn't speak because there was nothing to say. It had been what they'd agreed from the start...no ties.

But one of them had discovered that they didn't want it to be like that any more and it hadn't been him. She'd fallen in love with him, totally and for all time, and to find him back in Glenminster and part of her working life was going to take some adjustment.

Whether Drake's life had changed since then or not, she didn't know. But hers certainly had, because now there was Poppy. Poppy was the small bright morning star that Tessa had adopted after getting to know her while she'd been in the children's ward in Horizons. On the strength of that, Tessa had done two of the things that they'd vowed to steer clear of all that time ago: allowed a child into her life on a permanent arrangement and taken out a mortgage.

She had moved out of the apartment where she'd lived and loved so passionately, bought a cottage built of golden stone not far from the hospital and life had been good again because there'd been love in it. A different kind of love, maybe, but love nevertheless.

Drake was standing by the window of the hotel room, gazing out to where theatres and restaurants were sending out a blaze of light onto the main street.

In the background was the everlasting drone of the traffic that would be far more noticeable when daylight came, and was a far cry from the silence of the mountains and the soft white snows of Switzerland.

But his yearnings weren't for those. He'd left Glenminster without a second thought three years ago with an easy mind, because Tess had seemed willing enough to keep to the pact they'd made on the night they'd met.

So why was it, he asked himself, that the moment his contract in Switzerland had come to an end he'd caught the first London flight available to be there for the meeting? And why had he hired a car to take him directly to the place where they'd lived and loved until his ambition had come between them?

It wasn't like he'd been expecting Tessa to be all dewy-eyed and panting to take up where they'd left off three years before. If he had, she would have soon put that misconception right when she'd seen him at the meeting and observed him so joylessly that the attention he'd been receiving from everyone else had seemed claustrophobic.

If she was going straight home in the morning, would she let him give her a lift? he wondered. For all he knew, she might be turning the occasion of the AGM into a shopping trip or a theatre break and he could hardly go knocking on her bedroom door to question her plans after three years of silence and all that had passed between them...

He had planned on making an early start because he had to find somewhere to live when he got to Gloucestershire. He wanted to be settled into some kind of accommodation before appearing at the hospital in his new role on Monday morning. So it would seem that unless they met at breakfast their first proper encounter would be at work, under the eagle eyes of their colleagues. It was hardly ideal, but they were professionals and they would make the best of it.

It turned out that Tessa was already in the dining room amongst a smattering of other early risers when he went downstairs at six o'clock the next morning, and before he could give it another thought he stopped by her table and said, 'I've got a hire car and will be leaving shortly. Can I give you a lift to Gloucestershire?'

'No, thanks just the same,' she told him levelly, in the process of buttering a piece of toast. 'I have a seat booked on an early train. The taxi that I've arranged to take me to the station will be here soon.'

'Are you still at the same address?' he asked casually, letting the rebuff wash off him.

'No, I've moved recently,' was the curt reply, and then to his surprise she followed up with 'If you haven't got any accommodation arranged, there is the house in the grounds of the hospital that the retiring consultant has been living in.

'The property was bequeathed to Horizons in the will of some grateful patient and is now vacant. I'm sure it could be made available to you if you wished.'

Drake was frowning. 'I don't want any fuss, Tessa, I'm here to work.' He realised his tone had come across perhaps a little harshly, so he added, 'But I suppose living so near work could be very useful.'

In truth, he was amazed. After her tepid reaction to his return he hadn't expected her to do him any favours. He was the one who'd been a selfish blighter all that time ago and anyone observing them now would find it hard to believe they'd been lovers.

'I will most certainly look into that,' he assured her, dragging his mind back from the past.

Meanwhile, Tessa's only thought was whether

there would be anyone sharing the place with him if it was available.

It was an old house that its previous owner had cherished, with high vaulted ceilings, curving staircases and spacious rooms all furnished with antique objects, with its biggest benefit being that it was only a matter of minutes away from the hospital for the consultant in charge when needed.

'Now that you mention it, I seem to remember something about being offered it when I accepted the position,' he said, 'but I had so much on my mind at the time I'd completely forgotten about it. So thanks for that, Tessa.' Could he sound more like an idiot? Drake thought to himself.

She shrugged as if it were of no matter. 'You would have heard about it sooner or later.'

'Yes, well, thanks anyway,' he told her, and as a member of the dining room staff came to show him to a table, added, 'Until Monday morning, then.'

She nodded and turned back to her tea and toast, hoping that she hadn't given any sign of the fast-beating heart that the turmoil inside her was responsible for. Having already settled her account, when her taxi arrived she left the hotel as swiftly as possible, and without a backward glance.

So far so good, Drake thought sombrely as he watched her go. At least they were on speaking terms *and* Tessa had taken the trouble to tell him that his accommodation arrangements might soon be solved. But who was it that *she* had moved house for?

She wouldn't have left her beloved apartment

for no reason, and he could hardly expect that her life had been on hold while he'd been away. She'd watched him leave that day without a murmur. Or could it have been that he hadn't given her a chance to get a word in with his obsession about the job in Switzerland, and the opportunities for developing new techniques it had presented?

But he'd made his choice and paid the price. It had been over then and nothing had changed. It wasn't like he'd returned to Horizons for her. He'd wanted the job—and to see her for old times' sake, not to rekindle what had once been between them.

But that wasn't to say that he'd forgotten the passion they'd shared, or how it had felt to lie in each other's arms. So much so that he hadn't slept with anyone since, hadn't found anyone he'd wanted to share that with. Now that he had some distance, he could see that what they'd had was without equal— but he didn't regret taking the Swiss job, which had developed his skills and offered him a once-in-a-lifetime opportunity. Now, for better or worse, he was back and he couldn't deny that a part of him was curious to see if there was anything left of it.

He could tell from Tessa's manner that his return hadn't sent her into raptures—far from it—but perhaps beneath her frosty reception she was as curious as he to see whether any of the old passion remained. The old Tessa certainly would have been.

On the train journey home Tessa rang her friend Lizzie, who was Poppy's childminder and the only person she would entrust her adopted daughter to stay with overnight, and was told that she'd been fine. A little bit weepy at bedtime but a couple of stories had made her eyelids start to droop and then she'd slept right through the night.

'I should be with you by lunchtime and will come straight to your place,' Tessa told her, but Lizzie suggested bringing Poppy to the station to meet her, knowing how she would be longing to see her again. Tessa was anxious to hold her little girl in her arms again, and thanked Lizzie, who was mother to two cute little ones of her own. But when her friend asked if the meeting had justified the long journey and overnight stay in London, Tessa could only reply that it had been full of strange surprises.

She didn't regret refusing Drake's offer of a lift home, even though it would have been faster. The thought of being in close contact with him for three to four hours had been inconceivable.

Until yesterday he had been out of her life completely and now he'd come back into it with the same ease as when he'd appeared at her door at six o'clock in the morning an eternity ago, and now she was wishing him far away... Or was she?

With Drake back in her life he would no longer be a shadowy figure from her past. She would be able to see him and hear him, but would also have to keep him at a distance.

Her life had been transformed with Poppy in it. The little one had been in care, waiting to be adopted after losing her parents in a car crash, and when she'd been brought into Horizons soon after with a bleed behind her eye from the accident, Tessa had been drawn to the solemn little orphaned girl and had spent much of her free time beside Poppy's bed.

'*You* are just what the child needs,' her social worker had said.

'What! A single mother!' she'd exclaimed. 'Hardly! My life has never been planned to include children.'

But the seed had been sown and the more she'd thought about it the more she had known that she wanted to take care of Poppy. So the proceedings to adopt had begun, with every step along the way feeling to Tessa more and more that it was the right thing to do. If she needed any confirmation of it, the happy little child that Poppy had become was proof.

If Drake had any recollection of the pact they'd once made, he was in for a surprise, she thought, and as the train left the station on the last leg of her journey home she was wishing that he had stayed in the place that he'd been so eager to go to, because now she had her life sorted.

They were waiting for her on the station platform, Lizzie holding Poppy's hand tightly as the train stopped, and when she saw her, the little one cried, 'Mummy Two!' It was the name that Tessa had taught Poppy to call her so that 'Mummy One' wasn't forgotten, and as she held her little girl close her world righted itself.

'So where are the boys?' she asked Lizzie, whose twins were the same age as Poppy.

'They are at home with their daddy. He's taking a few days' leave from work so I didn't need to bring them,' Lizzie explained, as she pointed to where her car was parked. As they walked towards it she asked, 'So what went wrong while you were in London, Tessa? You didn't sound very happy when you phoned.'

'You aren't going to believe it when I tell you,' she told her. 'Guess who is taking charge at Horizons from Monday?'

'I haven't a clue. Who is it?' she asked.

'Drake is to be the new chief consultant. Drake Melford!'

'What?' Lizzie cried. 'He's back here in Glenminster? How do you feel about that?'

'Honestly, I'm shattered at the thought. My life is sorted, Lizzie. I'm happy as I am with Poppy and my job. They fill my days.'

'Have you actually spoken to him?'

'Yes. He's on his way here in a hire car and offered me a lift, which I refused…needless to say.'

'And he's taking over on Monday?'

'Yes, giving me no time to compose myself after our London meeting,' Tessa replied, looking down at Poppy, who was holding her hand tightly, 'but nothing is going to interfere with my life and Poppy's. Drake will be in my working life—that I can't help— but for the rest of it he will be just as much out of it as he has been during the years we've been apart.'

* * *

Her first thought on awakening on Monday morning was that she would be in the same place as Drake today. Indeed, it was a while before she could focus on anything else. For not only would she be in the same place as Drake *today*, she would be for the foreseeable future. While their professional goals would be aligned, she could imagine him making his entrance into the life of Horizons Hospital with his usual charm and confidence, while she would be struggling just to keep afloat.

But at least she wouldn't be on the wards or in Theatre, where he would surely be. That would be intolerable, so if the chance came to stay in her office all day she would take it. *Coward*, she couldn't help but think.

What about all the other days when she would be out there, arranging and improving the standard of care that the hospital provided for its patients? She couldn't hide in her office every day.

She'd risen through the ranks because of her expertise, efficiency and professional manner. She had years of experience, having worked in a similar capacity on cruise ships, and wanting to revert to dry land for a change had gone into hospital administration. She couldn't help but wonder how her life would have been different if she'd never met him, if she'd stayed on cruise ships perhaps.

But there was no point going over what couldn't be changed. And, anyway, she could never regret the road that had brought her darling Poppy into her life.

Her friend Lizzie lived on the other side of the hospital, at the edge of a town that was endowed with the beautiful architecture of bygone days and wide shopping promenades. It was an arrangement that suited both mothers. As well as putting Tessa's mind at rest, knowing her little adopted daughter was cared for by someone she could trust during working hours, it provided Lizzie with an income of her own and gave the two friends an excuse to see each other very often.

Tessa had to drive past the hospital to get to Lizzie's and as she took Poppy to be dropped off she saw what must have been the hire car that Drake had indicated when he'd been offering her a lift at the London hotel.

It was parked amongst other staff cars and she wondered where he had stayed over the weekend, and how she could possibly be so disinterested after the way she'd adored him. Had her feelings eventually turned to pique because she'd been discarded so thoughtlessly for a promotion and a trip to Switzerland?

When she arrived at her office, which was part of the hospital's administration complex, her secretary, middle-aged Jennifer Edwards, was already there and eager to inform her that the new senior consultant had called to say hello on his way to the wards and what did she think of that?

'I don't think his predecessor even knew we existed,' Jennifer said in a tone of wonder, and Tessa's hopes of a busy day in the office without sightings of Drake began to disappear. But Jennifer went on to say that he'd stopped by to explain that he was calling a meeting of *all* staff who were free to attend at five o'clock that afternoon and hoped that the two of them would be there.

'But will you want to stay behind?' she asked Tessa, knowing that normally she would be setting off to collect Poppy at that time.

It was a tricky question. Her dedication to her job demanded that she be there to support the new head consultant, and deep down she knew that if it wasn't Drake she would be phoning Lizzie to explain that she would be a bit late. She'd already been away from her little one for part of the weekend on hospital business and felt that she had given enough of her free time, but Tessa knew that was just an excuse. It would be worse if Drake thought she was being difficult because he had come back into her life unexpectedly—perhaps she should go to the meeting just to show him that he was fine. *Stop it, Tessa*, she told herself severely.

She was free of the spell he had cast over her. And she wasn't going to the meeting. If they didn't speak today she would explain tomorrow that she'd had another commitment that had been equally important.

It had been a hectic day, Drake thought, as he made his way to the main hall of the hospital at five o'clock, but it was to be expected with patients and staff all new to him…with the exception of one.

Would Tessa be there when he spoke briefly to his new team? He hoped so. There was no way he would want to cause her pain or embarrassment, but they were adults—and professionals, for goodness' sake—and could surely behave that way.

If his restlessness and discontent while he'd been in Switzerland had been because he'd made a big mistake by not cementing their relationship, there was nothing to indicate so far that *she*'d been missing *him*. If she was now living with someone else, he had only himself to blame.

He was crossing the hospital car park to get to where the meeting was being held and caught a glimpse of her in the distance, about to drive off into the summer evening. He quickened his step but she was pointed in the opposite direction and as the car disappeared from view he had his answer.

She had better things to do, it would seem, than stay behind to hear his few words of introduction to the staff. It was going to take more than just showing up, or his charm, to get to know her again. Did he even want that?

Minutes later he faced a varied assembly of the workforce and with complete sincerity assured them that every aspect of the day-to-day challenges that Horizons Hospital was confronted with would have his full attention. Relieved that the meeting at the

end of their working day had been brief yet reassur-
ing, most of them went on their way, leaving just a
few who wanted to meet the new chief consultant.

CHAPTER TWO

AFTER THE LAST of the staff members had left Drake's thoughts turned to food.

He was starving, and the thought of relaxing over a meal in a good restaurant in the town centre had no sooner surfaced than he was on his way there.

He had to pass a park on the way and happened to cast a glance at a certain bench that had memories of a time that was as clear in his mind now as it had been then. Did Tessa remember? he wondered. Did she think of it each time she passed this spot?

As he drove along a country lane not far from the hospital he unexpectedly found his curiosity satisfied about where she had moved to. It was in the porch of a cottage by the wayside that he saw Tessa, and he almost ran the hire car into the hedgerow in his surprise.

She was chatting to a guy of a similar age to himself and as he drove past Tessa reached out and hugged him to her. Drake's first thought was that this had to be the man who had replaced him in her heart. His second thought, which took a while to

summon up, was, So what? But at least he knew now
where she was to be found out of working hours.

As for himself, he'd wandered into the house in
the hospital grounds that she'd mentioned, after remembering the keys on his desk and the chairman's
note offering him the use of it, and thought it wasn't
his type of place. It was too drab and he thrived on
light and colour. But he had already decided that its
proximity to Horizons would be perfect in an emergency, so was going to take advantage of the offer.
He'd look for something else when he had time.

The food was fine when he found a restaurant that
was his type of place; it battened down his hunger
with its goodness, but Drake hardly noticed it. He'd
got the job of a lifetime back in his home town and
a place to sleep that plenty would die for, yet he
wasn't happy.

It had been a mistake to come back to where he
and Tessa had been so besotted with each other, so
right for each other in every way. He'd had three
years to realise in slow misery that he'd thrown away
a precious thing without a second thought to satisfy
his ambitions, and would have been even more selfish if he'd expected that time might have stood still
where she was concerned.

She was just as beautiful now as she'd been then,
but there was no warmth in her towards him, and as
the night was young—it was barely seven o'clock—
he decided to call on her on the drive back. If possible, he would wipe the slate clean by apologising

for his past behaviour and assure her of his intention
to stay clear, with the exception of their inevitable
coming face to face sometimes in a professional capacity at Horizons.

When Tessa opened the door to him the shock of
what he was seeing rendered him speechless. Standing behind her on the bottom step of the stairs and
observing him unblinkingly was a small girl in a
pretty flowered nightdress with hair dark as his own
and big brown eyes.

'Who is *she*?' he questioned, standing transfixed
in the doorway.

'She's my daughter,' Tessa told him. 'Her name
is Poppy.'

'How old is she?' he asked hoarsely.

'Three.'

There was a pause. 'Is she mine too?' he asked in
barely a whisper as the colour drained from his face.

She shook her head and watched the dark hazel
of his eyes become veiled. 'Who *is* her father, then?'
he choked, as the small vision on the bottom step
rubbed her eyes sleepily.

'Poppy is my adopted daughter,' she told him.
'Her parents were killed in a car crash and we got
to know each other when she was brought into Horizons with a bleed behind her eyes from the accident.

'She was with us for quite some time and we became close. I used to sit beside her whenever I got
a spare moment and take her a little surprise every

day. In the end I applied to adopt her and was successful. So there you have it. No cause for alarm.'

Turning, she scooped Poppy up into her arms and
held her close. As their glances met she told him,
'Poppy has brought joy into my life.'

'Yes, I'm sure that she must have,' he said flatly,
turning to go. But then thought that before he did he
might as well ask another question that could have a
body blow in the answer. 'So is the guy I saw leaving earlier her new daddy?'

'No, of course not,' she replied, her voice rising at
the question. 'There are just the two of us and we're
loving it. The man you saw was the husband of my
friend Lizzie who minds Poppy while I'm at work.
When I picked her up this evening we left her doll
behind, and he brought it, knowing that she would
be upset without it.'

'Ah, I see,' he said, and added, with a last look
at the child in her arms, 'I'll be off then, to let you
get on with the bedtime routine and maybe see you
somewhere on the job tomorrow.'

'Yes, maybe,' she replied.

She was relieved to see him go. Her heartbeat was
thundering in her ears, her legs were weak with the
shock of his surprise call, and she didn't know how
she was going to cope with having Drake so near yet
so far away in everything else. He probably thought
she was crazy to be taking on the role of mother to
someone else's child.

As he walked down the drive to his car she

couldn't let him go without asking, 'Did you find somewhere to stay?'

He turned. 'Er, yes. The keys for the mausoleum, along with a welcoming note to use it if I so wished, were waiting for me, and as it's so near where I'm going to be working, and I didn't feel like looking for anywhere else, I took advantage of the offer.'

'You don't sound too keen on the accommodation,' she commented.

'It's a roof over my head, I suppose, but it's rather dark and dreary. I'm more into light and colour, if you remember.'

She remembered, all right, remembered every single thing about him from the moment he'd knocked on her door early one morning until the day he'd packed his bags and left. But the memories had been battened down for the last three years and she wanted them to stay that way.

He had his hand on the car door and as he slid into the driving seat and waved goodbye, she carried a sleepy Poppy up to the pretty bedroom next to hers. Looking down at her, the feelings that being near him had brought back disappeared as her world righted itself again.

Tessa didn't sleep much that night. She usually went to bed not long after Poppy to recharge her batteries for the next day, but not this time. Her moments of reassurance when Drake had gone and she'd carried Poppy up to bed hadn't lasted.

She kept remembering how his face had changed

colour from a healthy tan to a white mask of dis-
belief when he'd thought that Poppy was his, and
when she'd told him that she wasn't, she could tell
that he'd thought she was crazy to adopt a child.
Clearly nothing had changed with regard to what
he saw as *his* priorities, and they obviously didn't
include parenthood.

Why did he have to come back into her life and
disrupt her newfound contentment? she thought dis-
mally as dawn began to filter across the sky.

In her role as health and safety manager Tessa went
round the wards each week, chatting to patients at
their bedsides about what they thought of the food,
cleanliness and general arrangements of the famous
hospital, taking note of any comments that were
made. The morning after Drake's surprise visit it
was down as her first duty of the day.

As she made her way to the children's ward,
where it would be parents she was chatting to rather
than the small patients, one of the nurses who had
been there when Poppy had been admitted caught
her up on the corridor and asked when she was going
to bring her in to see them.

The plight of her small adopted daughter had
pulled at all their heartstrings when she'd been admitted frightened and hurt after the car crash that
had taken the lives of her parents. But Tessa had ex-
perienced a strong maternal feeling towards the little
orphan that had made the promises she and Drake
had made to each other seem selfish and immature.

At that time she'd had few expectations of ever seeing him again, but she'd been wrong and thought guiltily that she should be happy for the hospital's sake that he had taken over, instead of complaining about the effect he was having on her life.

'I'll bring Poppy the first chance that comes along,' she told her. 'It is just that the days seem to fly.'

On the point of proceeding to wherever she was bound, the nurse said, 'What about Drake Melford? Wow! If I wasn't so fond of my Harry I'd be tempted. That man is every woman's dream!'

He was certainly that, Tessa thought, and when she looked up the man himself was moving quickly along the corridor in their direction and the nurse made a swift departure.

She felt her shoulders tensing, but then reminded herself it was Drake the surgeon coming towards her, not the dream lover of the past, and with a brief 'Hello, there,' he was gone.

Drake had driven the short distance back to the hospital car park the night before in a state of amazement. The scene he'd just been confronted with at Tessa's cottage had revealed that the person she'd moved house for was a parentless child, a small girl without a father. *He* could hardly get his head around what was certainly the last thing he'd expected to find on his return to Glenminster.

A husband and a child of her own wouldn't have been too much of a surprise, but the dark-haired

little tot at the bottom of the stairs had been nothing less than a shock to his system, and after seeing
Tessa in the corridor just now, he had to admit that
he was still reeling.

She had done the rounds of patient appraisals and
been closeted with the laundry manageress for the
rest of the morning. Then, after a bite of lunch, she'd
spent the rest of the day in her office, dealing with
the demands of the busy eye hospital, and it wasn't
until Tessa was leaving at the end of the day to go to
collect Poppy that she saw Drake again on his way
to Theatre. He nodded briefly in her direction, but
instead of accepting thankfully that it was a sign he
was keeping the low profile that she wanted from
him, Tessa was filled with sudden melancholy.

It came from the memory of strong passions and
their fulfilment in a relationship that for her had
been transformed into a love that was strong and
abiding, and not according to the promises they'd
made to each other when they'd first met. If she'd
told Drake back then how she'd felt he would have
seen it as not keeping to her part of the pact they'd
made and so she'd stayed silent.

And now when he had finished for the day, whenever that might be, he would be alone in the huge
house that he had reluctantly opted for, while she
would be alone in her living room, Poppy asleep
upstairs. It was a matter of minutes between their
respective homes, but an unimaginable distance in
every way that mattered.

Why couldn't he have stayed away, she thought anxiously as she set off to Lizzie's, instead of coming back to awaken memories from the past that she'd finally been able to put aside because her life had been made liveable again since she'd adopted her precious child.

She'd seen his expression when she'd explained who Poppy was, as he'd observed her at the bottom of the stairs, and he'd actually gone pale.

Yet there was no one better than Drake for bringing a smile to the face of a frightened young patient in the children's clinic, having them laugh instead of cry while he was making a shrewd assessment of their problems.

They'd been in a similar professional situation when they'd first met. He'd been on the staff of a less famous place than Horizons but had been moving up the ladder fast, already a name that was well known in the profession, and she'd been employed as a mid-level manager where she was now, which had brought her into his line of vision when he'd been the speaker at Horizons that night.

His had been a personality that had drawn her to him like a magnet. From the moment of their meeting she had been enraptured, and, being just as much a free spirit as he was, had thought that the pact they had made would survive any hazards or setbacks.

But lurking in the background had been his ambition, his determination to be at the top of his profession, and he'd gone and left her to pick up the pieces, taking her silence on the matter as her acceptance of the open-ended arrangement they'd agreed on.

Tessa had been thankful they hadn't lived together, had each kept their own space, that there had at least been one aspect of his going that she hadn't been left to face.

As days had turned to weeks and weeks to months she had felt only half-alive until Poppy had become part of her life and her own unhappiness had seemed as nothing compared to what had happened to the little orphaned girl.

When she arrived at Lizzie and Daniel's to collect her after each working day, she felt joy untold to hold her close and know that she was hers.

'So how has another day with Drake around the place gone?' Lizzie questioned when she arrived.

Her friend had been there for her during the long months after his departure, and knowing how much Tessa had been hurting, she had admired her when she'd adopted the small girl that she was holding close.

'Not bad' was the reply. 'I've seen him briefly a couple of times but not to talk, so I guess he's getting the message.'

'And are we sure that it is the right one?' Lizzie questioned, raising an eyebrow.

'Yes,' she was told firmly.

'Good for you, then. He hasn't brought anyone with him…maybe a wife or fiancée?'

'It would appear not,' Tessa told her, and went on

to say, 'I haven't told you, have I, that when Drake called last night and saw Poppy, he asked if she was his. Something that would never have been on his agenda, and he seemed quite overcome with relief to be off the hook when I explained that she wasn't.'

'So nothing changes, then?'

'No, it would seem not. And now that he's taken over at Horizons I'm just grateful that I'm not on the wards or in Theatre. With my job our paths won't cross that much.' She smiled and took a breath. 'He's living in the big house in the hospital grounds at present and not liking it all that much, which I can believe. He is too much of a socialising sort of person to enjoy living on his own in that sort of place, but once he gets into his stride we shall be seeing the real Drake Melford.'

Later that evening, sitting alone in the cottage garden with Poppy fast asleep upstairs, Tessa was watching the sun set over the hills that surrounded the town in a circle of fresh greenery and letting her mind go back to that other time when its golden rays had embraced her and Drake on their last night together.

She'd vowed then that never again would she leave herself open and vulnerable to that sort of pain and loss, and had kept to it, relying on a polite but firm refusal when other men had sought her company.

There had been no expectation in her to hear from Drake again so she hadn't been disappointed.

But a part of her was still hurt that he hadn't even dropped her a quick line to let her know how the new job was going, if nothing else.

Then out of darkness had come light. Poppy had come into her life and she'd begun to live and love again, and nothing was going to interfere with that, she vowed as the sun began to sink beneath the horizon.

On Saturdays she took Poppy to see her maternal grandfather in the town centre. Tessa had met him at her bedside when the little girl had been brought into Horizons after the accident, and had been aware of his frustration at the thought of his granddaughter being taken into care because he was too old to look after her.

When Randolph Simmonds had heard some time later that the smiley blonde hospital manager loved Poppy and wanted to adopt her, he had been overjoyed and looked forward to their weekly visits.

He had an apartment in a Regency terrace overlooking one of the parks not far away from the town's famous shopping promenades, and always on Saturdays insisted on taking them out for lunch and afterwards driving them up into the hills, where pretty villages were dotted amongst the green slopes.

Randolph was due for eye treatment soon in Horizons and his first question when they arrived on the Saturday was whether the new fellow had arrived yet, as he wanted Drake Melford to be in charge of any surgery that might be necessary.

'Yes,' Tessa told him. 'He has been with us a week, but, Randolph, you need to be on his waiting lists, or do you have an appointment to see him privately? Drake is extremely busy.'

'Oh, so it's Drake, is it?' he said, twinkling across at her. 'You're on first-name terms?'

'I knew him way back before he was so much in demand, though he was already making a name for himself,' she explained flatly. 'I hadn't seen him for quite some time until the other day.' Then she steered the conversation on to a different topic. 'Do you want me to sort out an appointment for you privately? Or you can see him through your optician or GP, if they think it is necessary.'

'You could make me a private appointment if you would,' he said immediately. 'I'm getting too old to be shuffling around waiting rooms and clinics.' With his glance on Poppy, who had gone out into the garden to play, he asked, 'How is the little one? Does she still cry for them in her sleep?'

'Not so much,' she told him. 'I've taught Poppy to call me "Mummy Two" so that your daughter isn't forgotten, and she seems happy with that.'

'And maybe one day there might be a "Daddy Two", do you think?' he questioned.

'There might, but don't bank on it,' she told him. 'The three of us are happy as we are, aren't we?'

He sighed. 'Yes, you were heaven-sent, Tessa.'

When they went for lunch to Randolph's favourite restaurant Tessa was dismayed to see Drake seated at one of the tables. But, she thought, having already promised to speak to him on Randolph's behalf, and not looking forward to any kind of one-to-one discussions with him, it seemed an ideal opportunity to put forward the old man's request.

'Isn't that the man himself?' Randolph exclaimed. 'I saw his picture in one of the local papers.'

'Yes, that's him. I'll introduce you while he's waiting to be served and you could mention an appointment now if you like,' she said, as they approached his table.

'Yes, why not?' he agreed.

Drake had seen them. He rose to his feet as they drew near and Tessa saw that his glance was on Poppy, who was holding onto her grandfather's hand and looking around her.

'This is a surprise, Tessa. I wasn't expecting to see you here,' he said, with a questioning smile in Randolph's direction.

She ignored the remark and changed the subject by saying, 'Can I introduce Randolph Simmonds, Poppy's grandfather?'

As they shook hands the old man said, 'We have just been discussing my need for a private appointment with you, sir, which Tessa was going to organise, and here you are.'

It was a table for four and Drake pointed to the three empty seats and said, 'Why don't you join me for lunch and tell me what it is that you want of me.' Beckoning a nearby member of staff, he asked them to bring a child's chair for Poppy.

Tessa felt her heartbeat quicken. This wasn't what she'd expected, but there was nothing she could do about it now, and while Poppy's grandfather was engaged in explaining his eye problems to Drake she talked to Poppy and pretended that she wasn't shaking inside.

Until Drake's voice said from across the table, 'I've just been explaining to Mr Simmonds that I'm going to do as my predecessor did before me and use the same facilities that he had put in place for his private practice in the big house in the grounds. So, yes, I will ask my secretary to get in touch with him first thing on Monday morning, if that will be satisfactory.'

This is ludicrous, he was thinking. Across the table from him was the woman he'd once romanced and made love to in a torrent of desire and had had it returned in full, and they were behaving like strangers. But he'd forfeited the right to anything else and was now paying the price. It was hellish, making polite conversation when he'd adored every inch of her way back in what seemed like another life.

Fresh menus were being brought to the table for the extra diners and as Tessa gazed at the selection of foods available the print blurred before her eyes.

She would have the fish with the creamed potatoes and fresh vegetables, she told them when they came for her order, with a child's portion for her daughter.

Once they had eaten they would go their separate ways, and this would all be over. But soon it seemed that, like everyone else who met Drake, the old man had fallen under his spell and wanted to chat.

Yet Randolph had no problems about them moving on when she made the suggestion at the end of the meal, but to Tessa's dismay Poppy had. She had wriggled down off her chair and gone round to the other side of the table, and climbing up onto Drake's knee was sitting there, sucking her thumb. After a moment of complete astonishment on his part, his arms closed around her.

This is madness, Tessa thought wildly. Not only was Randolph impressed by Drake's easy charm, but her beautiful Poppy must be seeing in him something she hadn't seen in any other man since she'd lost her father. It had to be him of all people, him, for whom babies and mortgages were no-go areas.

Drake was reading her mind as clearly as if she was speaking her thoughts, and putting Poppy gently back onto her feet he led her back to where Tessa was sitting and said softly, 'Yours, I think.'

'You think correctly,' she told him levelly, 'and now, if you will excuse us, Poppy's grandfather always takes us up into the hills when we've had lunch, don't you, Randolph?'

'Er, yes,' he replied uncomfortably, and turned to their host. 'It has been good to meet you, Mr Melford. Maybe next Saturday *we* could take *you* for a meal, if you aren't too busy.'

Tessa noted that he didn't say either yes or no, just smiled, and she thought, Please, let it be a no when next I see him.

When they were clear of the restaurant Randolph asked curiously 'So what is it with you and the man back there, Tessa? What have you got against him? I thought he was most pleasant. We butted into his mealtime with our requests and interruptions and he never batted an eyelid.' He looked down at Poppy's dark curls. 'Whatever *you* might think of him, our young miss took to him like a duck to water.'

'Yes,' she admitted. 'I saw that. It is just that Drake and I had a misunderstanding a few years ago.'

'And you still bear a grudge?'

Not a grudge, she thought. It was scars that she carried, mental and physical ones, but she wasn't going to tell Randolph that, so she just let a shrug of the shoulders be the answer to that question, and he let the matter drop.

Randolph was very fond of both Poppy and Tessa, whose loving role of a second mother to his grand-daughter took away some of the dreadful feeling of loss that he had to live with, and no way did he like to see her unhappy in any way.

But as he drove the last stretch homewards he was reminding himself that all he knew of her was what he saw now, in her early thirties and beauti-ful. There had to have been men in her life previ-ously, if not at the present time, and it seemed that Drake Melford might have been one of them, though clearly not any more.

* * *

When the little family had left the restaurant after the uncomfortable moments when Poppy had been drawn to him, Drake sat deep in thought. It had been a mistake to come back to where his roots were, and where he'd had the mad fling with Tessa. Yet what was it he'd been expecting when he did? That nothing would have changed and Tessa would be waiting, patient and adoring, after the abrupt way their affair had ended?

One thing he certainly hadn't expected was that she would have a child in her life. Not his, of course, not a child born of a 'no responsibilities' type of guy, but a sweet little thing that it would be easy to love, given the chance.

He'd liked her grandfather, had been relieved to see that there was someone else connected with Tessa and the child. Whatever the old man's problems with his vision, he would give him his best attention when he came to see him, and with the thought of an empty weekend ahead he paid for their meals and went to see what was on at the theatres and cinemas in the town centre.

There was nothing that appealed and on a sudden impulse he drove to the place not far away where he had lived when he'd met Tessa.

It was an apartment in a block of six and if it had been up for sale he would have bought it for the sake of the memories it held, and to get away occasionally from the big cheerless property in the hospital grounds.

Seeing that it wasn't on the market, he turned the car round, drove back the way he'd come, and settled down for the night in the mausoleum once more.

Back at the cottage Tessa was wishing that they hadn't come across Drake in the restaurant and that she hadn't suggested that Randolph should speak to him about an appointment, because if none of that had happened Poppy wouldn't have gone to sit on his knee and given *her* food for thought.

She had been content in her new life until that moment, but now the future seemed blurred instead of clear, and Randolph hadn't enjoyed their time together so much after that because she hadn't been able to face telling him the truth about how she'd come to know Drake Melford.

CHAPTER THREE

SATURDAYS SPENT WITH Randolph were pleasant and relaxing, but Sundays were precious, when Tessa had Poppy to herself all day. She did chores in the morning while her small adoptive daughter played with her toys, and in the afternoon they went to the nearby park, where they picnicked either inside or out, according to the weather.

Again Tessa hadn't slept. She'd twisted and turned restlessly as the memory of their meeting with Drake in the restaurant had kept coming back to remind her that it had been a crazy and intrusive idea to confront him with Randolph's request for an appointment.

But as usual he had brought his charm into play and come out of it on all sides as the relaxed and understanding host who had been swift to hand her child back into her keeping. An apology from her was going to be due when next they met which would be at the hospital in the morning. That was her last thought before the patter of tiny feet and a

small warm body snuggling in beside her indicated
that breakfast-time was approaching.

As the day followed its usual pattern Tessa began
to relax. Worries of the night always seemed less in
stature in the light of day, she decided as she drove
to the park on the edge of the town.

She'd parked the car and as they walked the short
distance to the children's play area she was hoping
that she might have a day without any sightings of
Drake.

Her wishes were granted. The day passed happily, as it always did, except for the fact that she
couldn't help wondering what he was doing in his
absence. One thing she felt certain about was that
he wouldn't be spending the time in his over-large
accommodation if he could help it.

But Tessa was wrong. He was doing just that because he wanted the arrangements for seeing private
patients to be sorted for Monday morning, with a
secretary installed. Especially after the request he'd
had from Mr Simmonds the previous day.

He was still bemused by his meeting with the
three of them, especially with little Poppy's entrust-
ing climb up onto his knee, and if he hadn't been so
aware of Tessa's dismay he wouldn't have handed
her back to her mother so quickly.

By the time he had finished rearranging part of
the house he was hungry but resisted the urge to
dine in the town again. He knew it would afford a
glimpse of Tessa's cottage on his way there, as well

as a sighting of a certain park bench, so he took a ready meal out of the house's well-stocked refrigerator and made do with that.

During a long night spent amongst creaking boards and the smell of mothballs he'd decided that, after looking up Poppy's case notes from the time Horizons had treated the eye injury she'd sustained in the car crash, he was going to suggest to Tessa that he should check her over to make sure that all was well with her vision and the surgery that she'd had.

It wasn't anything to do with how he'd felt when the little girl had climbed up on to his knee. It was his job for heaven's sake, to bring the far horizons closer to those who might be denied the sight of them.

On his very first morning there he'd been faced with a child that he might never be able to do that for. A five-year-old boy with an eye missing, born with just an empty socket, had been there for a regular check-up, and if it hadn't been so sad it would have been amusing the way he could remove the artificial eye he'd been fitted with and put it back with so little fuss at such a tender age.

If there had been no sightings of Drake during Sunday it seemed that he was making up for it on Monday morning, Tessa thought when she arrived at the hospital. No sooner had she positioned herself behind her desk than he was there, observing her with a dark inscrutable gaze that made her heart beat faster.

But there was no way she was going to let him see how much he still affected her. It was different from her wild passion of before—now she saw him more as a threat than a joy, jeopardising the new life she'd made for herself with Poppy. As she observed him questioningly, what he had to say took her very much by surprise.

'I've had a look at your little girl's case notes,' he said without preamble, as if he had guessed the direction of her thoughts. 'Would you like me to check the present state of her vision and the area where she had the surgery to make sure that all is still well there?'

'Er, yes,' she said slowly. It was an offer she couldn't refuse for Poppy's sake. Drake was the best, but she didn't want to be in his debt in any way, didn't want any relighting of the flame that she had been burned with before she'd learned the hard way that what they'd shared had meant nothing to him.

She often thought that if they'd spent less time making love and more getting to know each other in the usual way of new acquaintances, if she'd got to know his mind before his body, she could have been saved a lot of hurt and humiliation.

But maybe that was how Drake liked his relationships to be, and if that was the case there was no way she was ever going to let him know the degree of her hurt when he'd taken thoughtless and uncaring advantage of the pact they'd made after those first magical moments.

Tessa doesn't trust me with her beautiful child, he thought. Can it be that the little one coming round to my side of the table to sit on my knee in the restaurant on Saturday is rankling?

'You don't sound so sure,' he commented, turning away as if ready to leave. 'It seems about time she had a check-up, just to make sure all is still well with her vision.'

'I'm sorry if I sounded dubious about your offer,' she told him awkwardly. 'It was just that you took me by surprise. Yes, I would be grateful to have your opinion about Poppy's vision and anything that might be going on behind her eyes. So far she's had a clean bill of health regarding that, but I do worry sometimes.'

'Then do I take it that you will trust me on that?' he wanted to know.

'Yes, of course I will,' she told him hurriedly, and wished that their conversations were less overwhelming.

'Good. I'll get my secretary to ring you to arrange a time when you and I are both free for me to see your child.'

'She does have a name!' she said dryly. 'I suppose you think I'm crazy adopting Poppy after all that we vowed?'

'I'm not in a position to be making judgements,'

he replied, 'but as far as that's concerned it's clear to see that you're happy in the life you have chosen, that you have no regrets.' *Which is more than I can say for myself*, he thought. And then, from nowhere, he found himself saying, 'It would be nice if I could take you for a drink somewhere, for old times' sake.'

'I don't go out in the evenings,' she said, her colour rising at the thought.

'You haven't got a childminder, then? What about your friend Lizzie?'

'Lizzie sees enough of me and mine, and after being away from Poppy in the daytime I want to be where she is in the evenings.' With her cheeks still flushed at the thought of being alone with him, she continued, 'My life these days is very different from when I knew you. It has sense and purpose and...'

'All right!' he said. 'You don't have to justify yourself, Tessa. It was only that I thought it would be nice to bring ourselves up to date with each other. How about I buy you lunch one day in the hospital restaurant if you don't want to spend time away from your child? Not very exciting, I know, but it might be more convenient for you.'

'Yes, of course,' she said, smiling across at him, and thought there wouldn't be much time for chatting if they did that, which would suit her fine. The last thing she wanted to accompany the meal was memories of the good times they'd had blotting out the misery of how it had all ended.

At that moment her secretary came bustling

into the outer office, ready for the week ahead, and Drake departed, striding purposefully back to the ward.

When he'd gone Tessa felt like weeping. Since Drake had arrived at Horizons he hadn't had a moment to spare from his consultancy, yet he'd taken the trouble to check Poppy's records and offer an appointment.

It was only in his attitude to his private life that she'd ever found him to be less than generous, but she had known the risks that came from that sort of affair. If only she hadn't been so mesmerised by him, and remembering his startled questioning about whether Poppy was his when he'd seen her that night at the bottom of the stairs, she wondered what his reaction would have been if she'd had to tell him that she was.

Would he have been horrified at the responsibilities that would have come with her and dealt with them from afar?

Jennifer in the outer office was fidgeting to get started on the day ahead, so putting her mind games to one side Tessa called her in and the mammoth task of keeping the hospital clean, hygienic and well supplied with food and clothing began.

Meanwhile, somewhere else in the picturesque old stone building that had once been a wool mill Drake and his staff were preparing to perform what would have been impossible in bygone days, and as he scrubbed up for whatever surgery lay ahead after his stilted conversation with Tessa he would have been grateful for a minor miracle of his own.

If she had shown distress at the thought of him leaving her behind all that time ago he might have taken notice, but the euphoria he'd felt at being head-hunted by the Swiss clinic had made him oblivious to things around him, and apart from her being a little quiet and withdrawn during his last few days everything had seemed normal. If she *had* said something, would he have taken notice with his head so high in the clouds?

The time he'd spent in Switzerland had been the coldest and loneliest he'd ever known. The experience and knowledge he'd gained over the three years had been excellent, but he hadn't been able to stop thinking about Tessa and the magic they'd made together, which he'd cast aside as if it had been nothing.

When the position at the Horizons Hospital had been his if he wanted it, he'd accepted the offer without a second thought.

He hadn't flattered himself that time would have stood still for her, had accepted that she might have someone else in her life, but had never expected it to be a child that she'd adopted. He had to admire her for that, while at the same time shuddering at the thought of what it would entail.

As Tessa was on the point of leaving at the end of the day he rang her office and said, 'Sorry to be last minute with this, Tessa, but I haven't had a moment all day. It's just a thought, but how about your daughter coming to be checked over on Saturday? I've given Mr Simmonds an appointment in the morning and have accepted his invitation to have lunch with you folks afterwards. So if she's at all apprehensive, maybe her having watched my treatment of him will help to stop her from being upset. What do you think?'

'Er, yes, I suppose so,' she said hesitantly, with the feeling that since his surprise appearance he already featured too much in her life. She went on to say, 'Although Poppy does know you already, doesn't she?' And isn't afraid of you...and I'm not looking forward to another uncomfortable meal, she thought in silent protest.

He almost groaned into the earpiece and said, 'I'll leave it with you, but it would be better from both our points of view if she came on Saturday as my time on weekdays is soon filled', and rang off.

When she arrived at Lizzie's her friend said, 'You're looking very solemn.'

Tessa dredged up a smile. 'Ashamed would be a better description. Drake is being kind and thoughtful and I'm as prickly as a hedgehog when I'm in his company. He's offered to check Poppy's vision and the back of her eye where she had the bleed just to make sure that all is well there, and—'

'Surely you didn't refuse?' Lizzie exclaimed.

'No, of course not, but I wasn't gushing, and he wants me to take her to Horizons on Saturday morning while her grandfather is having a consultation with him to reassure her if she isn't happy about him doing some tests.'

'I don't see anything wrong with that,' Lizzie said gently.

'No, neither do I.' she agreed, 'except that I feel as if he's too much in my face.'

'And you definitely don't want that?'

'It's a matter of my not being able to cope with it, but obviously I'm not going to refuse anything that's beneficial to Poppy, so when she's asleep tonight I'm going to phone him and accept his offer.'

Randolph rang in the middle of Poppy's bathtime and while she splashed about happily he informed Tessa that a secretary had been on to him, offering an appointment with Dr Melford on the coming Saturday morning, and he'd accepted it with pleasure.

'So that's good, isn't it?' he said. 'And she informed me that he's pleased to accept our invitation to dine with us when the consultation is over. I hope that's all right with you, Tessa, as I know you're not a member of his fan club.'

'Drake has offered to check Poppy's eyesight along with any scarring from the bleed she might have and will generally give me an opinion on the state of her vision,' she replied. 'He wants me to bring her to the clinic on Saturday so that she can watch him examining your eyes, and hopefully she won't be too fretful when it's her turn. Needless to say, I'm most grateful for the offer but that is all. After what Drake has done for you and Poppy I can hardly refuse to join you for lunch. But, Randolph, please don't expect me to be the life and soul of the party on Saturday.'

'So the rift runs deep, then,' he said disappointedly, and having no intention of explaining just how deep it was she left it at that.

She didn't tell him that she hadn't given Drake a definite answer regarding Saturday because in spite of his thoughtfulness in offering to check Poppy's eyes she still felt as if she couldn't communicate with him.

But for her little one's sake she would accept his offer, and take her to his consulting rooms at the same time as Randolph.

When he'd gone off the line and Poppy was asleep Tessa sat deep in thought as the summer dusk that would soon be tinged with autumn colours fell over the town and its surroundings. She'd been so happy in her newly found contentment, she thought as she looked around her. Why couldn't Drake have stayed away?

But if he had it would have been Horizons that would have been the loser, as well as herself, and she couldn't wish that on the patients in need of a specialist eye hospital who lived in Glenminster and the surrounding areas.

She was just going to have to keep a low profile where he was concerned—as if she wasn't doing that already. And if it got to be too difficult? Well, she would just have to move somewhere else where he wouldn't be always under her feet as a reminder of a time in her life that she'd once wanted to last for ever.

When she finally rang Drake there was no reply, so she concluded that he must be eating out somewhere, and for the briefest of moments she let memories of the past, the passionate never-to-be-forgotten past that had left her hurt and aching for him, intrude into the present. But then the sight of Poppy sleeping the sleep of the innocent brought calm to her stressed mind.

When she phoned again and said that Saturday morning would be fine for her to bring Poppy for a check-up he said, 'That's good. If she watches me with her grandfather first, she should be happy enough when it is her turn.'

'Er, yes,' she said hesitantly, and waited for a comment about the four of them doing a repeat of the previous week's lukewarm meal together, but there wasn't one coming, so maybe she was exaggerating its importance.

When she told Lizzie about Drake's suggestion, that they catch up for old times' sake, her friend said, 'So what do you think it means, that he's sorry about the past? Or that he's just trying to mend fences with a colleague?'

'He did refer to the past while we were discussing it,' Tessa told her. 'A mild comment along the lines of why didn't I say something if I wasn't happy about him leaving, But we'd agreed that it was to be a no-strings affair and he'd been so on top of the world about Switzerland I think he would still

have gone, even if we'd been in a proper relationship.' She sighed and finished with, 'So, as far as
I'm concerned, Lizzie, nothing changes, and that's
how I want it to stay.'

When Saturday came Tessa dressed with care in a
blue linen dress and jacket and shoes with heels instead of her working flatties.

She had dressed Poppy in a pretty pink dress with
shoes to match and as the minutes ticked by she
could feel tension rising inside her at the thought of
what lay ahead. But it was also bringing back memories of how badly hurt Poppy had been, orphaned
and injured, and those first moments of seeing her
when word had been going around the hospital about
her plight.

There was also the thought that the morning's
events were everything she'd been trying to avoid
with Drake as much as possible. An eye examination for Poppy, yes, but dining with him afterwards
was a different matter, an ordeal to be faced, and
the sooner it was over the better.

There had been no signs of any long-term after-
effects of the bleed and bone fracture, but to have
him—of all people—check that all was well behind
those beautiful dark eyes had been something she
couldn't possibly have refused and as she and Poppy
watched while he dealt with Randolph's vision, they
were all making light of it for her daughter's sake.

But not enough, it seemed. When Tessa would
have settled on the chair that he had just vacated

with Poppy on her knee she rebelled, and sliding down, said, 'You first, Mummy Two.'

When she seated herself reluctantly into a make-believe position in front of Drake and his instruments she saw amusement in his glance. This wasn't part of the arrangement!

'Don't touch me,' she said quietly.

'Of course not. I have no intention of doing any such thing,' he said smoothly. Pointing to nearby instruments, he said, 'These are what I will be using, my hands don't come into it, but that isn't going to persuade your daughter to do what we want if she's set against it, unless I can rustle up some of the charm that I keep on hand for this sort of fraught occasion.

'But first we have to convince her that you are also having an eye test.' He raised his voice. 'So put your chin on the ledge in front of you, Tessa, and look straight into the green light for me.'

It worked, and after watching Drake actually giving her an eye test Poppy came over, climbed up onto her knee and allowed him to do the same thing for her. When it was over and Tessa had lifted her down and sent her to sit by Randolph, he said, 'I've looked at the backs of her eyes, Tessa, all is well there, and her vision is excellent too.'

He was serious now, amazingly so, very much the ophthalmologist instead of the ex-lover as he said, 'I'll write you a report and let you have it first thing on Monday if you'll come to my office before my day gets under way.'

'Yes, of course,' she told him. 'Thank you for giving us your time this morning, Drake, and I'd like to settle your account at the same time on Monday if you will have it ready then.'

'There's no rush,' he said absently, with a frown across his brow as if his mind was elsewhere, and she hoped he wasn't going to use the occasion to bring them back onto a better footing.

'So, are we ready to eat now?' Randolph was asking. 'I've booked a table at one of the restaurants on the promenade.'

'Yes,' Tessa said, watching mesmerised as Poppy went to stand beside Drake and put her hand in his.

Aware of her reaction, he looked across, shrugged his shoulders and followed Randolph to the car park of the hospital, leaving her to bring up the rear with a strong feeling that the meal ahead was going to be exactly the nightmare she'd feared.

As they neared the cars he said, 'Obviously, I haven't got a car seat for Poppy, so if she stays with you and Mr Simmonds, I'll follow on behind.' The glint in his eyes told her that he could read her mind, but what was she supposed to do when her adorable child made a beeline for him?

'So Poppy's eyes are good, then?' Randolph said, turning to Drake as they were shown to a table in one of the town's best restaurants. 'That's a relief, isn't it, Tessa?'

'It certainly is,' she agreed, and was ashamed of her reluctance to sit down to eat with the man who had given them such welcome news. For the rest of the time she let her gratitude show by smiling across at him whenever their glances met, but wasn't rewarded by any warmth coming from Drake's side of the table. Just a brief nod in her direction was all that was on offer.

The answer to his strange behaviour was waiting for her when she presented herself at his consulting room on Monday morning. 'I have something to tell you that you won't like,' he said levelly, when she'd seated herself across from him, and he watched dread drain the colour from her face.

'You've found something wrong with Poppy's eyes after all?' she questioned anxiously.

'No, she's fine,' he told her reassuringly.

'So it's Randolph who has a problem?' she questioned as relief washed over her in a warm tide, knowing that he would rather it was him than anything happen to his granddaughter.

'No, all he needs are a couple of cataracts removed,' he said sombrely. 'It's you that I'm referring to. It was fortunate that I gave you a proper eye test, instead of pretending for Poppy's sake, as it has shown an eye defect that may need surgery.'

'Me!' she gasped. 'That can't be right, surely!'

'I'm afraid it is,' he said levelly.

'No,' she said, fear rising inside her. This was what single mothers must dread, she thought, not being there for their child when the unexpected threw their lives into chaos. All right, Lizzie would look after Poppy for her if she was hospitalised, but it wouldn't make it any less agonising to be away from her.

As he observed her dismay Drake thought that her eyes, as blue as a summer sky with golden lashes, were one of the things he remembered so clearly from their time together. During the test his attention had been drawn to the fact that on one of them the pupil had been forcing her eyelid apart, which was an indication that there could be over-activity of the thyroid gland—also known as hyperthyroidism.

As he explained the situation, pointing out that it was a problem that could restrict eye movement and cause double vision, Tessa's pallor deepened and her dismay increased as he went on to say, 'Sometimes it can be solved by medication to relieve the pressure, but it isn't always successful and then surgery is required to bring the vision back to normal. But first I need to arrange some tests.'

'And will I have to be hospitalised if I need surgery?' she asked tightly.

'For a short time, yes,' was the reply, 'but you can always go somewhere else if you don't want to be treated here.'

'Of course I want to be treated here!' she protested, and as her voice trailed away weakly she added, 'By you.'

'Fine, so under the circumstances I am going to treat you myself while the relevant clinics do their bit, and with regard to that will take some blood from you now to go to the endocrine folks for testing. The results should be back by tomorrow morning and when I get them I will know better what I am dealing with. Have you not noticed any discomfort in and around your right eye?'

'Er, yes, I suppose I had,' she told him. 'It felt tight in the socket, but not enough to cause alarm as I haven't had anything like double vision, but I don't have much time to fuss over myself. My world revolves around Poppy.'

Drake longed to take her in his arms and tell her that he would make it all right for her, that he'd been a prize fool to have left her like he had, and since he'd found her again was aware of the depths of her hurt.

But he knew that a few hugs and kisses wouldn't wipe out the past, the decisions they had both made, and the awkward situation they now found themselves in. Even though Tessa had said she wanted him to perform the surgery if the need arose, he knew that she didn't want him in any other part of her life. How did he feel about that, especially now she had a daughter? He shook his head at the thought. How had a simple affair between co-workers become this complicated?

'Be prepared to make yourself available first thing in the morning Tessa, and we'll take it from there,'

he'd told her, and she'd nodded with the feeling that they were being thrown together whether she liked it or not. But there was also relief, a warm tide of it inside her, because Drake of all people would be there to see her through the nightmare that had just unfolded in her life.

'I have to get back to the office,' she said weakly.

He nodded. 'Yes, of course, by all means. I'll give you a buzz in the morning when I have the results of the blood test and Tessa, don't worry, I will be with you all the way'.

It seemed as if she had no reply to that, and nodding she went back to her daily routine with a heavy heart. What was happening to the contentment that she'd cherished so much, she wondered miserably as she sat hunched behind her desk.

First Drake had come back to stir up the past that she'd thought lay buried deep, and now she might need surgery. But there was one happy thought that came to mind. He'd said that Poppy's vision was fine and Randolph's would be too once the cataracts had been removed.

So with those comforting thoughts and the knowledge that whatever was wrong with her eyes was going to be treated by the top ophthalmologist for miles around, she had to be grateful that he had come back into her life, if only for that.

About to start his Monday morning clinic, Drake was imagining the kind of thoughts that must be going through her mind. How cruel a twist of fate that he should have to tell Tessa that she had a problem that might be serious, on top of everything else still unresolved between them. Yet there was relief in him too, because it was sheer luck that he had been examining her eyes and had therefore spotted the problem early. There was every chance that it could be treated without the need for surgery.

Still hunched behind her desk, Tessa was reminding herself just how much expertise there was under Horizons' roof, how dedicated these medical professionals were in treating those who relied on them. Whatever her personal feelings towards Drake, nothing could compete with that. So as calm settled on her she called Jennifer into her office and began to face the day's duties, doing her part to look after the health and safety of the hospital and its patients.

When she called at Lizzie's that evening to pick Poppy up it was her first opportunity to tell her the results of their Saturday morning appointment at the clinic with Drake.

'So everything is fine, then,' she said delightedly, when she heard what Drake had said about Poppy's eye test, but her expression sobered on hearing of Tessa's problem She held her close and told her, 'Between us we'll cope. Daniel and I will look after Poppy if you're hospitalised, and this time Drake will be doing what he does best and not disappearing into the sunset. But, Tessa, how do you feel about seeing him so often, about having him feature so much in your life? Do you still have feelings for him?'

She shook her head. 'Not really, but now that I've got some of the hurt out of my system I remember how fantastic it was, being loved by him. Drake appeared in my life from nowhere and went out of it just as quickly.

'Knowing him, his stay at the hospital might be brief now that he's in my company once again. He won't want to be confronted by an old girlfriend everywhere he turns, and I don't want to be reminded of how I became surplus to requirements when Switzerland beckoned.'

Back at the hospital Drake had just finished for the day and was making his way towards his accommodation with little enthusiasm. What to do during the evening, he wondered. A boring ready meal and then an early night was what it would most likely be. He'd had a few of those of late and had lost the taste for them.

His mind kept going over those fraught moments with Tessa. It was typical in the present climate between them that he should have to take the sparkle out of her life with the news about what might turn out to be a worrying problem, with the only good side to it being that *he* was going to be in charge of it.

That was how he saw it, but in spite of her appearing to be happy about the arrangement he'd known that to her it would be just a means to an end, that the sooner it was sorted the sooner her fears that she might be separated from Poppy would be gone. If he could promise her *that*, she might just let him into the life that he now had no part in. But was that what he wanted, especially on such terms?

If ever she let him back into her life he would want it to be because it was him she needed, not his expertise.

In such cases as Tessa's, medication was usually tried first to slow down the over-activity of the thyroid gland. Surgery was only resorted to when it didn't solve the problem, and if he could save Tessa the stress of an operation he most certainly would. Not only because he cared about her as a patient but because he cared about her for old times sake…

CHAPTER FOUR

AFTER PARTAKING OF the inevitable ready meal, Drake felt restless. It was a clear, calm evening. The sun was about to set over the town and the hills that encircled it, making him feel stifled inside the big house. It had been another hectic day and he needed a break. So, prescribing himself some fresh air, he set off to enjoy what was left of the day.

What would Tessa be doing at this time? he wondered, and leaving the hospital behind he walked towards the town. Would she be sitting alone in the cottage while the little one slept up above, with the news about her condition lying heavily on her and no one to discuss it with?

He would be there in a flash if he thought she would welcome it, but at this point he ought to consider himself lucky that she'd agreed to let him treat her. She had been quite willing to hand over Poppy and her grandfather into his care, but he hadn't known what to expect when it came to herself.

The cottage would be coming into view soon and if he had any sense he would pass it without stopping. But sensible he was not, because he found himself pressing the doorbell within seconds of it appearing in his line of vision.

It wasn't opened to him and, restraining himself from going round the back in case Tessa had seen him and didn't want to be disturbed, he went on his way, shaking his head at how disappointed he felt. It stood to reason that she was inside as small children were usually asleep by the early evening, and there would be no opportunity for lie-ins for that small family, with her having to take the little one to her friend's house every weekday before going to the hospital. Why she had lumbered herself with that kind of responsibility he really didn't know.

When they'd met up again a part of him had hoped they might fall back into the easy agreement they'd had before he'd got his values all mixed up. But it was turning out to be a lesson in endurance because there were no signs that she still had feelings for him. Instead, a small brown-eyed, dark-haired child was bringing Tessa more happiness than he ever had.

He was passing the park once again, but this time his glance fell on a group of parents watching over their small offspring in the children's play area. Amongst them was Tessa, looking pale but composed as she pushed her child backwards and forwards on one of the swings.

She hadn't seen him, but Poppy had and she was indicating that she wanted to get off the swing. When she'd lifted her down Tessa glanced up and saw the reason why. It looked like she didn't know whether to be happy or sad, but there were no signs of any inward tumult as she greeted him.

'I called at your place as I was passing and got no answer,' he told her, 'and now I know why.' Poppy held out her arms to be picked up. 'Isn't it somewhat past the young miss's bedtime?'

'Yes and no,' Tessa told him, as he bent to lift the small figure up into his arms with a wary glance at her mother. 'Lizzie said that she'd had a long sleep this afternoon and wouldn't be ready for bed at the usual time so we came out here for a breath of air and some play time for her. Why was it that you called at the cottage?'

'Just to check that you were all right after the upsetting news I had for you earlier today. But now that I've seen you and am reassured, I'll be on my way.'

He put Poppy gently back on her feet and when she was standing firmly said, 'I've been in touch with her grandfather today, and I'm going to remove one of his cataracts some time next week.'

'You didn't tell him about *my* problem, I hope,' she said. 'If Randolph gets to hear about it he'll start concerning himself about my not being there for Poppy as he's too old and frail to take on the responsibility.'

'Of course I didn't tell him,' he told her dryly. 'I would have thought that you would have been around hospitals—and me—long enough to be assured of patient confidentiality. At the moment he doesn't need to know anything as tests need to be done on your eye first.'

His glance was fixed on what lay behind her and she knew why. The bench where they'd once made love in the moonlight when the park had been empty was in view.

'Don't even think of it,' she said in a low voice.

'Why not?' he questioned, 'You're asking me to forget something as special as that?'

'Special for who?' she asked, and when she took Poppy's hand in hers and began to walk away he didn't stop her, just watched her go and continued his walk into the town grim-faced.

With no reciprocation from Tessa regarding the pleasures of the past, Drake brought his thoughts to the treatment of her condition. If it was an overactive thyroid gland that was affecting her eye; it might react satisfactorily to medication, but didn't always. If it didn't work and surgery was needed because the pressure in the orbit area was so severe that it was restricting the blood supply to the optic nerve, possibly leading to blindness, it would become a more serious matter. He had no doubt that Tessa would have read up on it by now and must be tuned in to what lay ahead, so he could imagine just how much she would want some definitive results on the situation, for her child's sake more than anything else.

Back at the cottage, with Poppy now asleep beneath the covers in her pretty bedroom, Tessa was allowing herself some moments of reflection. If she and

Drake had been together in the way that they'd once been, and Poppy had been their own child, it would be so much easier to face up to this thyroid thing, she thought bleakly.

But in the present situation she was using him because of who he was—the top man for eye problems in the area—knowing that there was none better. Part of her was imagining it as payback time, when the truth of it was that Drake owed her nothing. He had merely kept to the pact they'd made and had moved on when the Swiss job had come up. Could she really blame him for that?

And now he was back, having gained the expert reputation that he'd sought so eagerly. It was fine, just as long as he hadn't any ideas about taking up with her where he'd left off. It was too late for that. Her life was so different now, she had different priorities and a casual no-strings hook-up couldn't be further from her mind.

The next morning there was a message waiting for her in the office asking if she could spare him a moment. When Tessa explained to her secretary that she would be missing for a while and would Jennifer proceed with the routine of the day in her absence, the older woman was surprised but asked no questions.

She found him seated behind his desk like a coiled spring, ready to face the day's demands. But he was clearly prepared to put her first amongst his commitments as he said with a keen appraisal of the offending eye, 'How are you feeling this morning?'

'Not on top of the world,' she said flatly.

'I can understand that. How is Poppy?'

'Happy. She loves going to Lizzie's to play with her twin boys, who are a similar age,' she told him, and wished he would leave out the small talk.

As if he'd read her mind Drake said, 'I have the results of the first blood test.'

'Yes?' she questioned anxiously.

As she faced him across the desk, what he had to say was both was good *and* bad. Aware of the distance between them, and how different it was from the intimacy they had once shared, he needed to tread carefully because he knew just how much she didn't want to be in his debt in any shape or form, yet she was having to rely on him because he was the most senior eye surgeon at Horizons. Their past only complicated what should have been a purely professional relationship, and he couldn't let it affect the care he would be giving her.

'Your thyroid gland has become overactive,' he said, 'and that is causing the swelling of the eye socket, which could be dangerous if left untreated. In cases such as yours another doctor would normally be in charge of prescribing the medication to slow it down. But in this instance everything has to be centred on not interfering with the optic nerve. As I've already promised, I am going to deal with every aspect of the problem myself, and if there is no improvement over the next few weeks and the eye problem is worse rather than better, we must consider surgery.'

Aware of her distraction the previous day he said, 'I was sorry that I had to deliver such news, Tessa,' his voice softening. 'I'm tuned in to your opinion of me and all I can say is that protecting your sight will be my prime concern.

'At the sign of any further change in the eye socket please don't hesitate to get in touch. I'm available day and night and I have already sent down to the pharmacy for the medication that you will require. Someone from there will deliver it to your office.'

She was on her feet. 'Thanks for that, Drake,' she told him steadily. 'Needless to say, I will trouble you as little as possible as my vision isn't affected so far.'

With that she went, trembling after the attempt at calmness that she'd just presented him with, and praying that nothing would stop her from looking after Poppy.

When she'd gone Drake got to his feet. His busy day was waiting and nothing that was to come could possibly make him feel so concerned as the moments he'd just spent with Tessa. So much for a happy reunion. He must have been out of his mind for even thinking of it, but at least the fates had given him the chance to be there for her in her hour of need. For the present, what more could he ask?

He had longed to put his arms around her during the conversation they'd just had and hold her close to let her see that she wasn't alone in the moments of stress and fear that had appeared from nowhere, but he could imagine the kind of response he would have got. Tessa might have thought he was using her distress to hit on her. Aside from being professional misconduct, that couldn't have been further from his mind in that moment. She was a friend and colleague receiving bad news, that was all.

When she arrived at her friend's house that evening Lizzie was watching anxiously for her arrival and her first words were, 'Have you got the test results?'

'Yes,' Tessa told her, dredging up a wan smile. 'It is my thyroid gland that has become overactive and is causing the problem. Drake is going to try me on medication first. If it doesn't work it will mean surgery,' and went on to say with her voice thickening in an unexpected moment of yearning, 'I would have given anything for him to have held me close for a moment.'

Lizzie's eyes widened.

'No, I'm not weakening in my determination never to let him take me for granted again. I'm just so grateful that Drake is on my case.'

'Why don't you and Poppy stay here for the night?' her friend suggested. 'I don't like to think of you on your own after today's news. You know the spare room is always ready for visitors and when Poppy and the twins are asleep you and I could pop out for a change of scene. You need some light relief and Daniel will keep an eye on them.'

'Maybe you're right,' Tessa agreed. 'I need to unwind, and get what is happening into perspective. It will be a few weeks before Drake can clarify any improvement in my eye condition and until then I need to live as ordinary a life as possible. But I'm still in my work clothes, which are hardly suitable for going out.'

'We are the same size,' Lizzie said. 'You can have the run of my wardrobe if you wish.' And while the children were having their bedtime drink the two women went to see what would be suitable for Tessa to wear on her first night in the town for as long as she could remember.

It seemed strange to be out in the nightlife once again, she thought. It brought back memories of the time when she and Drake had lived it up there at every possible opportunity and then gone back to the apartment where they'd made love.

It was incredible how different her life was now, but she had no regrets. It had more purpose, more giving than taking and she was happy with that, not that it stopped her from remembering what it had been like to be romanced by Drake.

Where was he tonight? Tessa wondered as she and Lizzie approached one of the town's famous nightspots. The Bellingham Bar was a popular meeting place for those who liked to relax in pleasant surroundings with good food and a cabaret for anyone who liked that sort of thing.

It had been a favourite haunt of the two lovers and as they paused outside the place Lizzie said, 'Shall we throw away our cares for a while at Glenminster's top spot? Or will it upset you?'

'No,' Tessa told her. 'Having Drake back in my life is just coincidental, so why not? What about Daniel, would he want you in a place like this without him?'

'He wouldn't mind. Daniel knows I'm safe as long as I'm with you and anyway our marriage is solid.'

Lizzie's throwaway comment hurt for no accountable reason. Tessa guessed she was just feeling fragile and sensitive because of the difficult news. She refused to admit that she was affected by Drake's sudden return to Glenminster, and she couldn't regret the life choices she had made. Poppy was the best thing ever to happen to her and nothing, not even thoughts of Drake, would change her mind on that.

Without further conversation she led the way into the bar and looked around her, almost as if she was expecting to find him there. After all, he was appearing in every other aspect of her life. But there was no sign of him, and she pushed firmly from her mind her earlier desire to have him hold her in his arms and comfort her.

She wasn't to know that he had been round to the cottage to check that she was all right and on finding her missing was at that moment on his way to Lizzie's house to ask if they knew where she was.

He'd had to drive through the town centre to get there and was dumbstruck to see the two of them, smartly dressed, going into the Bellingham Bar as he was passing.

Before he'd had time to think about what he was doing—or indeed, to ask himself why—he'd parked the car and entered the bar. The thought uppermost in his mind was that Tessa wasn't exactly moping after the day's dark moments, and he was some fool to think that it would have been him that she would have sought out if she had been.

She was studying the menu with head bent when he stopped at their table. As his shadow fell across her she looked up, startled. 'Drake,' she breathed, 'where have *you* appeared from?'

'I've come from trying to find you to make sure you were all right,' he said dryly, 'but it would seem that I needn't have concerned myself. I'll leave you to what is left of the evening.' Then a thought suddenly struck him and he blurted out, 'Where's Poppy?'

'She's safe at my house with Daniel and the boys,' Lizzie hastened to tell him as Tessa sat speechless.

'Right, I see,' he commented, and went striding out of the place with every woman's glance on him except hers.

'Would you believe that?' Lizzie breathed. 'How could he have known that we were in here?'

'I don't know,' she said, 'Maybe he was passing and saw us outside on the pavement. I feel dreadful. He will have been working hard all day at the clinic but still took the trouble to drive out to check how I was feeling, and now finds me about to start living it up in this place. How embarrassing!' Tessa put her head in her hands and groaned. Could this night get any worse?

'Let's go home.' Lizzie said gazing around her as the tables were filling up with would-be diners. 'It was a mistake to come here, though seeing Drake was the last thing either of us would have expected.'

'You're early!' her amiable husband said, when they reappeared. 'What happened to the night on the town?'

'Drake Melford happened to it,' Tessa told him flatly. 'He'd been to the cottage to see how I was after him giving me the results of my test today, and of course I wasn't there.'

'Lizzie and I think Drake was on his way to see if I was here and when he saw us going into the Bellingham Bar he wasn't pleased to find me there instead of being at home having a quiet evening,' she said ruefully. 'Not that it's any of his business what I do or where I go. All my evenings are quiet and I'm happy with that, knowing that Poppy is sleeping in dreamland only a few feet away.' Lizzie nodded and squeezed Tessa's arm in support. 'But tonight was different, Daniel. I needed something to take my mind off everything and didn't want to be alone, brooding over it.'

When she went up to check on Poppy a few moments later and stood looking down at her sleeping child, Drake's questioning of the little one's whereabouts came to mind and she thought wonderingly that he'd sounded almost father-like in his over-zealous concern for her well-being.

If the next thing he did was take on a mortgage she would have to eat her words, but in the meantime she felt she owed him an apology. His thoughtful gesture had clearly caused him further fatigue at the end of his busy day. It was the least she could do after his numerous attempts to reach out to her, and his kindness towards her little family.

The next morning she rang his office several times and was told by his secretary that Drake would be in Theatre for most of the day and asked whether she wanted to leave a message.

The answer to that was definitely no. What she had to say wasn't for anyone else's ears. But say it she must, and the first opportunity came when Tessa saw him coming towards her in the main corridor of the hospital at the end of the day.

'I've been trying to get in touch with you,' she said, stopping in front of him, 'but I understand that you've been busy. So can I take a moment of your time now to apologise for last night. I'm so sorry that I wasn't there when you called at the cottage and for my rudeness in the bar. If I had known to expect you I would have been there.'

Tessa rushed on, hardly able to look him in the eye as she delivered her rehearsed speech. 'As it was, I was feeling really low when I arrived at Lizzie's house and she suggested that Poppy and I stay the night. When the children were asleep she came up with the idea that we should go into town for a change of scene and some night life—which is never normally on my agenda—and I suppose it was as we were going into the bar that you saw us.'

He was smiling. 'The main thing is that you were safe and *I* owe *you* an apology for being so abrupt when I saw you. Shall we call a truce and make up with a kiss?'

When she took a quick step back he laughed. Taking her hand, he opened a door nearby that led into a quiet rose garden that was rarely occupied, and once they were out of sight Drake tilted her chin with gentle fingers to bring her lips close to his and kissed her.

It was like coming in out of the wilderness, magical and blood warming for the first few seconds, until Tessa pushed him away and with pleading eyes said, 'Please, don't do this to me, Drake. I want a relationship that has substance, one that will last.'

'And ours didn't, of course?'

'No, it didn't,' she told him, holding back tears at the memory of those last sun-kissed moments before he'd gone out of her life.

Turning, she went back through the door and was gone. As he followed her at a slower pace he thought bleakly, So much for taking things slowly.

'Did you see Drake to apologise?' was Lizzie's first question when Tessa arrived that night.

'Yes,' she told her, having scooped Poppy up into her arms the moment she'd arrived. 'But it was a rather hotch-potch affair as he said it was all his fault. He took me into a rose garden at the side of the hospital and I was like putty in his hands.' She shook her head at the memory. 'But the thought of this little one and all she means to me brought me to my senses.'

'What does Drake think about you adopting Poppy?' Lizzie asked.

'I don't know. I can't think he approves but he hasn't said anything. I imagine that he thinks I'm crazy. Part of the pact we made was to stay clear of exactly these sorts of responsibilities and it would appear that his ideas haven't changed like mine have. No doubt he will think that adoption is even more of a trap than an ordinary family. But if he does he's missing so much.' And with that, Tessa gave her gorgeous little girl a hug and silently counted her blessings for the way things had turned out.

Back at the big house that was so not to his liking, except for its nearness to Horizons, Drake was sitting on the terrace at the end of another busy day, reliving the moments with Tessa in the rose garden.

He could have gone on kissing her, kept on kissing her over and over, if she hadn't pleaded with him not to, and it had brought him swiftly down to earth. They were living in different worlds, he thought, and for once it occurred to him that she must be far more content than him.

Tessa had gone into the town for the evening to try to clear her head, and had had to face his bullish interruption just as her night of freedom had been beginning, and yet, incredibly, *she* had sought *him* out to apologise for not being at the cottage when he'd called to check on her. She was different. Tessa seemed sorted, happy. It was starting to make him question a lot of the decisions he'd made way back.

His private life was a lot more carefree than hers, but much less happy. He'd taken one of the theatre staff out for a meal one night after they'd worked late and were both ready for some food. She'd reacted like most women did to his likeable charm and if he'd asked her back to his place he knew she would have been quick to accept which would have made her the first woman he'd slept with since leaving Tessa for Switzerland.

Ironically, the one he did want in his bed didn't want him. Her life wasn't the same as when he'd known her before, and if he wasn't content with what he had now, Tessa was happy with the life she'd chosen. This thought brought to mind the small Poppy's apparent attachment to himself.

Could it be that he resembled her father in some way and it drew her to him? One thing was sure, she was a sweet young thing with a loving mother and no way had he any right to interfere in that.

The sun was going down over the hills that he loved, with villages hidden amongst them that were graced by old almshouses and farms built from the beautiful golden stone that the area was renowned for.

Since returning to Glenminster, he'd never been

any further than the hospital and the town centre. He told himself it was because he'd been too busy at the hospital, but he knew deep down it was because the place was full of memories that had all of a sudden become uncomfortable to face.

So a notice in the staff restaurant announcing that the yearly picnic for staff and their families was to take place on the coming Saturday had Drake's interest immediately. The arrangements were that the coaches hired to take them to the picnic area would be waiting in the hospital car park at eight-thirty.

He hadn't mentioned it to Tessa as he'd thought she might run a mile if he told her he was thinking of going on the outing—he had discovered that she was its main organiser—but the yearning to be up there on the hills was strong and he decided that unless an emergency at the hospital occurred to prevent him, he would be there waiting for the coach like any other picnicker.

On that thought he went into the house towering behind him and climbed slowly upstairs to spend another night in the four-poster bed that graced the main bedroom with its creaking woodwork and the smell of mothballs.

Before Saturday there was Randolph's cataract removal to be done and on the morning that he was due at his private clinic Drake had a quick word with Tessa to find out how much the old guy knew about her eye problem.

'He knows nothing as yet,' she told him. 'I so much dread upsetting Randolph.'

'Yes, I can understand that,' he said, 'and if the medication does its job he need never know, but, Tessa, it's early days. There's no guarantee that it will, and then he will have to know.'

'So that will be soon enough, don't you think?' she said, and he had to agree.

'I wanted him to come and stay with Poppy and me at the cottage when the cataract has been removed,' she told him, 'so that I can supervise the drops that he'll need to have and make sure that he doesn't do any bending down. But he assures me that his neighbour in the next apartment has offered to do all that, and as she will be there all the time while I would have to be at work during the day it seemed to be the best idea. She will be making him a meal and looking after him generally, but I will call on my way home each night when I've been for Poppy to make sure that her grandfather is all right.'

'What did Poppy's father look like?' he asked.

'I've only seen a photograph obviously,' she told him, surprised at the question. 'He was quite tall, dark-haired, hazel eyes. Why do you ask?'

'Just curious, that's all,' he replied, and went on to question, 'Does she ever cry for her parents?'

'She did at first, but not any more. I got the impression that she was very much her daddy's girl, though she's not cried for him recently, and I've taught her to call me "Mummy Two" so that her birth mother, Randolph's daughter, isn't forgotten.'

'Yes. I see,' he said thoughtfully, with a glance at the clock on the wall of her office. 'He will be here any moment so I must go. If anyone asks for me, I'll be in my rooms over at the big house. Also, I'm coming on the picnic on Saturday so will you please book me a seat on one of the coaches?' He rushed on to add, 'If there's a problem with that, I shall get a bike and fetch up the rear.' Without giving her the chance to reply, he was gone, leaving her to question if his comment had been a threat or a promise.

She could imagine the expression on the face of the chairman—who always put in an appearance at the event—if he saw his top medic following the coach on a bicycle. It would seem that a ticket for the man who still made her heart beat quicken was going to be required.

But what was he up to? He surely couldn't want to spend time with Poppy—she knew how he felt about children. After that kiss in the rose garden… could it be her he wanted to see? Tessa shook her head. She had set him straight on that front. Perhaps he just wanted to be amongst the beautiful green hills to get away from work. Whatever the answer to that question, nothing had changed as far as she was concerned. Her life was sorted and it didn't include Drake.

CHAPTER FIVE

DRAKE SMILED WHEN he came back after dealing with the old man's cataract in his surgery room. There was a coach ticket on his desk with a note.

With the compliments of the picnic organiser.
A seat next to the chairman in the first coach.

He wanted to be seated next to her, he thought. Not beside someone who was going to talk about work all the way there and back. But Tessa had outwitted him, and when he strolled across to the car park on Saturday morning beneath what was promising to be a hot sun he found that the two of them, mother and child in matching sundresses, would be travelling on the last coach to leave, in order to round up latecomers.

As he went to greet them Drake saw that the chairman was already settled in the first coach and he sighed at the thought of joining him. But Poppy had seen him and was approaching fast, dragging

Tessa along behind her. He said with a wry smile, 'Thanks a bunch for seating me with his lordship.'

'It seemed the right thing to do,' she said blandly.

'To you maybe,' he said, patting Poppy's dark curls as she gazed up at him. 'Tessa, how long is this thing going to go on between us? I've got the message. You don't want anything to do with me because I treated you badly. I was a thoughtless, selfish clod, leaving you as I did, but you never tried to stop me, did you?'

'No, I didn't,' she said, 'because I kept to the agreement we'd made that it was to be a no-strings affair. So how could I protest when you wanted out? It was the way you did it, as if I didn't matter, as if I didn't even exist!' Tessa stopped suddenly, remembering where they were as one of the nurses came hurrying into view with her children. 'Here are my last passengers, Drake, so if you would please go to your seat we'll be off as soon as I've given the coach drivers the go-ahead.'

'Yes, sure,' he said, and watching him go Tessa thought that she must be insane not to want to him back in her life if that *was* what Drake had in mind after his long absence.

His ambition and career had taken him from her once already, and she hadn't meant enough to him even to discuss the possibility of them staying together, making it work long distance, let alone that she might go with him. He hadn't shown a moment's regret that what they'd had was over, and nothing—

not even his dedication to restoring the sight of the blind—was ever going to lessen the hurt.

As Poppy tugged at her hand for them to follow him she shook her head and lifted her daughter up the steps of the coach they were travelling on. When the latecomers had settled into their seats they were off, driving towards a day in the sun.

'And so how is it going for you at Horizons?' the chairman of the famous hospital asked as soon as Drake was seated next to him. 'No regrets?'

'No. None,' he told him, the vision of the woman and child he'd just left as clear in his mind as the long nights in Theatre and the over-subscribed clinics that were filled with sufferers desperate for better sight.

Only the other day he'd dealt with a woman who had been diagnosed with a blocked blood vessel behind one of her eyes that had been affecting her vision quite seriously. She'd also had a cataract that had been in front of it, and that was going to have to be removed before he could judge if better sight was going to be possible for the patient.

It hadn't had the look of one of his success stories, but she had accepted it quite sensibly when told that the surgery might give her better sight but that there was a real possibility that she might lose sight completely in that eye, and the answer to that would only be revealed when the procedure was completed.

As it turned out she had been fortunate, Drake thought. When she'd removed the eye covering the next day she had cried out that she could see—and therein lay his whole reason for living, as in his life at the present there was no other joy to be had.

'How do you like your accommodation?' was the chairman's next question.

'It's all right,' Drake told him, 'but at the first opportunity I shall look for something else, not so large and more modern.'

'Yes. I suppose that's understandable as you aren't married with a family to accommodate,' the other man said. Once again the vision of Tessa and Poppy came to mind, and Drake couldn't believe that his thoughts were running along those sort of lines, especially with regard to another man's child. It was totally opposite from what he'd always decided about being burdened with family responsibilities of his own, let alone those of someone else.

The picnic was to take place in the tea gardens of a hotel in one of the area's most attractive villages, and when the last of the coaches arrived at its destination Drake was waiting for Tessa and Poppy to alight, along with its other occupants. When she saw him the 'organiser in chief' groaned.

How was she going to be able to concentrate on ensuring that all those present enjoyed themselves if she was mesmerised by Drake's presence all the time? Tessa thought. And what about Poppy? Was she going to run to him, as she'd tried to do once already?'

'If you've got things to take care of, I'll watch

Poppy until you're free,' he offered. As her small daughter was already clinging to his hand it didn't seem like the moment to argue, so she gave a brief nod and went to check on the catering that she'd ordered and find out which chairs and tables had been allotted to them for the occasion.

When that was sorted she went to look for Drake and Poppy and found him pushing her to and fro on a swing in the children's play area. He hadn't seen her and for a brief poignant moment Tessa let her heart take control instead of her hurt and it was there, the feeling that the three of them were bonded together, when deep down she knew that it wasn't so.

He turned in that moment and unaware of what was in *her* mind let her see what was in *his*. 'Here you are,' he said teasingly, 'eager to make sure that I haven't run off with your precious child! Of course I knew it would be more than my life was worth.'

'You needn't have concerned yourself about my thinking that,' she told him. 'I haven't forgotten your views on family life.'

The slight edge of bitterness that he could detect in her voice made Drake swallow his next comment. He'd been about to surprise her with the memory of his casual remark about house-hunting to the chairman.

While she'd been busy he'd taken Poppy onto the field where the other children were playing and, incredibly, he'd found it! It was there, on the other side of the hedge, his dream house, in the last stages of

being built in the golden stone that he loved, windows everywhere, a terrace to sit on in the sun, at
least five bedrooms at a glance...*and it was up for
sale!*

He'd decided that when Tessa came to claim
Poppy he was going to go across to get a closer
look, let the perfection of it sink in, then find the
builder whose name and phone number were on the
'for sale' sign.

Knowing none of that, she wasn't amazed at the
speed with which he handed her child back to her,
as if he'd had enough and been reminded exactly
why he never wanted children. In fact, Tessa thought
nothing of it, Drake being far from sharing her joy
in parenthood.

When she and Poppy had disappeared amongst
the crowd of picnickers Drake went to get a closer
look at the house and discovered the builder was on
the site, about to finish for the day. As he appeared
around the corner of the house—his house, Drake
already couldn't help but think!—the man eyed him
questioningly.

'Can I have a look inside?' he asked.

'Yes, sure,' was the reply.

'Would you show me around, please?' Drake
asked him. 'But only if you haven't got a sale already.'

'I haven't,' he replied. 'Wait a second, don't I
know you from somewhere?'

'Only if you've had cause to visit the Horizons
Eye Hospital in recent days.'

'I have,' the builder told him, surprise at the co-incidence lighting up his face. 'But it wasn't for me. It was you who treated my lad when his eye was injured during a football match at school.

'We thought he was going to lose his sight, his mother and me, but you sorted it. Goodness! What are the chances? If you decide to buy this house, I will consider it an honour.'

'It's just what I've dreamed of,' Drake told him, 'and if the inside is as beautifully designed as the outside, we have a deal! I'm sure we can come to an agreement on the price.'

'Gee whiz!' the man exclaimed. 'How long have you been house-hunting?'

'No time at all,' Drake told him. 'This could be my first and last time, viewing a property.' Gesturing towards the front door, he said excitedly, 'Lead the way!'

The inside of the house was just as attractive as the outside and when the builder told him what he looking to get for the property, he said, 'You have a deal. I'll give you the name of my solicitor and any other details that you may require. Let's shake on it now.' The builder beamed back at him. 'How long will it be before the house will be ready to move into?'

'I'd say about a month,' was the reply. 'There are a few things that I want to do to achieve the results that I have in mind, and of course if you are going to buy it you can have your say about anything that you would like done. As soon as the contracts have been signed, the keys will be yours!'

They shook hands again on that and as Drake made his way back to the picnic area he wondered what Tessa would think of what he'd just done. Would she even be interested? The last time he'd been this crazy was when he'd knocked on her door in the early morning, having only met her briefly the night before; when she'd asked him in they'd made love and it had been wonderful.

They'd carried on from there with the no-strings agreement, the one that he realised now had been mostly his suggestion. Although it had left him with a get-out clause when he'd been offered the Swiss contract, he'd paid the price with three cold, miserable years to contemplate the mistake he'd made in letting Tessa go.

Now he was back where it had all started and she didn't want him near her. She had a child who was strangely drawn to him…and, even more unusual, he was equally attracted to the little Poppy. But Tessa was doing everything she could to keep him out of Poppy's life and he found he was oddly hurt by this, unexpectedly so.

He found the two of them enjoying picnic food at one of the tables, and as he looked around him he asked, 'So how is it going?'

'Fine,' she told him. 'This sort of event depends so much on the weather' She glanced at the sky above. 'And today is perfect, especially for the children.'

It had been a good day for him too, he thought,

finding the kind of house he'd always dreamed of, and being in a position to buy it. But the way things were, he might be rattling around in it on his own like a pea in a bottle.

At the end of the day, as they walked to where the coaches were parked, Drake said, 'I've spoken to Randolph a couple of times and he's due to see me again next week for a check-up on his cataract removal. He seems quite happy with what he's had done so far, which is a start.'

'Yes,' she agreed. 'I've called on my way home each day and it would seem that he is being so well looked after by his neighbour Joan, I can almost hear wedding bells.'

'Really! Well, they do say that it's never too late,' he commented dryly. But whether Tessa had the same feelings was another matter, and until he knew what the answer to that was he needed to tread carefully.

The first coach was ready to leave, with the chairman once more settled in his seat. As Drake prepared to join him he looked down at Poppy and she gazed back up at him and said, 'I want to go with *you.*'

'Our seats are on the other coach,' Tessa told her gently, but she didn't budge and the chairman called across, 'She'll be all right with us, Tessa.'

Observing the reluctance in her expression, Drake bent down and when his face was level with

Poppy's he said, 'No, sweetheart, you belong with Mummy. I'll be waiting when you get back.' And taking her hand, he placed it in Tessa's and went to his seat.

He was true to his word, and when the last coach arrived back at the hospital Drake was waiting, and as Tessa saw him standing there she felt like weeping for the three of them, Poppy for the loss of her parents, Drake for trying to bring back the past that was dead and buried, and herself because his nearness was affecting her the same as it had always done.

'What do you have in mind now?' he asked, as Poppy ran into his arms. 'Bedtime for the young miss? Going for a meal? Or an assisted tour of the mausoleum?'

'The first one, I think,' she told him. 'It has been a long day for a child of her age.'

'Yes, of course,' he agreed, 'but, Tessa, before we separate I hope you don't think I'm deliberately encouraging Poppy to want to be near me. I know it's the last thing you would want. Do you think it could be that she sees her father in me for some reason?'

'I really don't know,' she told him hurriedly, 'and it's been a long day, Drake. Maybe we could discuss it another time.'

'Yes, of course,' he agreed, and cautioned, 'Be sure to give me a buzz if you're getting low on your medication.'

As he turned to go, Poppy lifted her face for a

kiss and Tessa turned away. Did he remember the time when all his kisses had been for her?

Sunday once again was chores in the morning and the park in the afternoon, and from the moment they got there Tessa was watching for Drake to arrive.

She wasn't to know that his intention had been to join them until he'd been called into Theatre at eight o'clock that morning, on his one day off, to deal with the emergency treatment of a guy who had received serious eye injuries on a building site. As the hours dragged by with no sign of him, Tessa had to keep reminding herself that he hadn't said he would be in the park, so she shouldn't be disappointed when he didn't come.

Looking in the mirror that morning, she hadn't been able to see any change as yet in the protruding of her eye and, desperate for reassurance, had wished him near. It must be the reason why his absence was getting to her so much, she decided, and consoled herself with the thought that at least she hadn't had to put up with Drake gazing at the park bench.

As soon as he'd received the message about the injured man Drake had assembled the members of his team who were on duty over the weekend and by the time he'd arrived they had all been in position.

One nurse was monitoring the patient's blood pressure while another was holding his hand and trying to soothe his fears while at the same time warning him not to move his head while being examined or operated on.

Drake's assistant was hovering closely. He was young, intelligent and keen to follow in his footsteps, observing everything his mentor did and said. However, the sight of the man with both eye sockets bleeding being wheeled into their midst on a stretcher and transferred carefully onto the operating table had caused him to pale for a moment or two.

The theatre sister stepped forward and gently wiped the blood away, where possible, to allow Drake the space to use the ophthalmoscope to check for tearing of the iris, or ruptures of the sclera, which could cause collapse of the eyeball or even blindness.

The atmosphere in the operating theatre was tense when he told the patient, after examining both eyes, 'There is a retinal tear of the left eye, which isn't good, but it looks as if the macula is still in place, which is the main thing, and we are now going to sort that out.

'But the damage to your right eye is not repairable because there are ruptures of the sclera,' he said gently. After passing the ophthalmoscope to an older colleague, and then to his assistant for their observations, he told the man, 'All I can promise is that your horizons won't have disappeared completely.'

He rang Tessa in the late afternoon and knowing every tone of his voice she could tell that he was feeling low.

'What's wrong?' she asked.

'I've been trying to save the eyesight of a guy from a building site who'd had his head split open, blood all over the place, and couldn't see afterwards. The damage to one of his eyes was untreatable, and in the other one there was a retinal tear that we just managed to sort out before his vision became impaired.'

'Have you eaten?' she asked with a shudder.

'No. Why?'

'Do you want to come round and I'll make you a meal?'

'Are you sure?'

'Yes.'

'Then thanks, I'd like to. Is seven o'clock all right? I've got some notes to write up, and before that the family of the injured man want a word as they've only just heard about the accident.'

'Yes, seven o'clock will be fine,' she told him, and when he'd rung off she was left to ponder why she'd issued the invitation. Had it been because she needed him near to give her reassurance about her own eyes, or because she could sympathise with Drake's frustration at not being able to save the man's vision? Or was it simply because she wanted him near for a little while?

When he tapped on the kitchen window so as not to awaken Poppy with the doorbell, Tessa was in the kitchen, with steak grilling and an assortment of vegetables bubbling on the hob. When she let him in his hunger peaked at the smell.

'This will be the first decent bite I've had in hours,' he said. He was assailed with the memory that it had been something more physical than food that had always been his first thought every time they'd been together all that time ago. That and prestige. Yet his expertise hadn't been enough today to save that poor fellow's eye; the man's injuries had been appalling. It was a miracle he hadn't lost his sight altogether.

'I need to wash up before I eat,' he said, bringing his mind back to the moment on hand.

'The bathroom is at the top of the stairs and Poppy's room is next to it,' Tessa told him. 'Please don't disturb her. If she knows you're here she will be down in a flash.'

'I wouldn't complain,' he said laughingly.

'Maybe not, but I would,' she told him, 'and you know making friends with her doesn't exactly fit in with your no-family-ties resolution, if I remember rightly.'

'Neither does the huge responsibility that you have taken on single-handed fit in with yours,' he said, suddenly serious. 'Why, for heaven's sake?'

'I thought you were hungry,' she chided, ignoring the question. 'The food is ready.'

Drake was halfway up the stairs and wishing he'd kept silent. The truth of it was he envied Tessa her life and her child more than he would ever have dreamed possible.

A vision of the beautiful house he was going to buy came to mind and he hoped that he wouldn't feel as lost and lonely in it as he did in the one he was staying in at the moment. It was hard to believe Tessa and Poppy would ever live there with him as she appeared to be content in her cosy little cottage, and was showing no signs of wanting to get any closer to him than on that first day of their meeting at the AGM.

When he sat down to eat it occurred to Tessa that they had crossed another barrier by her inviting Drake to eat in her home. When he'd finished, the feeling was still on her as he said whimsically, 'I think I'll book into a hotel for the night to get away from the smell of mothballs.'

'I have a spare room that you can use if you like that I always keep ready in case of visitors,' she told him. 'I don't like to think of you driving into town looking for somewhere to sleep after the kind of day you've had.'

'Do you get many?' he asked.

'What, visitors? Oh, yes, they come in droves,' she said laughingly.

'Sarcasm doesn't suit you,' he said softly, 'or maybe what you've just said is correct.'

'Yes, well, you're quite capable of working that out for yourself,' she told him teasingly. 'So do you want to stay the night?'

As if, he thought, with her only feet away and memories of how it used to be pulling at him. But he was crazy if he thought Tessa might want him to be part of the new life she'd made for herself.

He'd come back to Glenminster and found that she had her life sorted, not with another man but with a little orphaned girl.

He'd been dumbstruck at the sight of the small, dark-haired child standing sleepily at the bottom of the stairs when she'd opened the door to him that time, and been staggered when Tessa had explained the circumstances of her being there. But he was getting more and more comfortable with the idea of Tessa *and* Poppy in his life, though he was no closer to understanding why that might be so.

She had gone into the kitchen and was clearing away after the meal she'd made for him. With her back to him, she wasn't aware of him approaching until she felt him plant a butterfly kiss on the back of her neck, and as she swung round to face him he held out his arms. Unable to resist, she went into them.

If it hadn't been for Poppy suddenly crying out above it would have been like all those years ago when he'd called at her apartment at six o'clock in the morning and taken her into the bedroom.

But this time it was different, Tessa thought as she withdrew herself from his hold. She was no longer free and easy, she had a child, a beautiful little girl who depended on her entirely, and to reopen the floodgates of her love for Drake was not what she was intending.

The crying up above was becoming louder and

moving towards the stairs she said, 'I think you'd better go, Drake. Poppy has little nightmares when the memory of the car crash comes back and she feels frightened but doesn't know why, so I hold her close and cuddle her until she goes back to sleep.'

Moving swiftly upwards, she paused and looking down at him said in a low voice, 'I forgot for a moment where my responsibilities lie. It was crazy of me to ask you to stay, just a mad moment, that's all.' And then she was gone in the direction of Poppy's sobbing.

As he closed the front door behind him and drove back to his own place he relived the moment she had walked into his arms. It had felt so right, until Poppy had cried out. How quickly Tessa had let him see that her child came first, he thought. As if he didn't know that already.

The days, weeks and months after Drake had gone to Switzerland had been the darkest time of her life, she thought as she gazed at the child in her arms, now sleeping with dark lashes sweeping down onto flushed cheeks. It was Poppy who had brought her out of sadness and into joy as they had each healed the other's hurts.

But tonight Drake's nearness had brought back the longing she'd thought she had under control, and when he'd kissed her neck it would have gone on from there if Poppy hadn't cried out. Her daughter's anguish had brought her back to reality she thought as she laid her gently under the covers, leaving the door wide open so she'd hear any further sounds.

* * *

Drake was back in the big house and sleepless with everything that had happened at the cottage starkly clear in his mind. The meal Tessa had made him, her offer of a bed for the night had taken him by surprise, considering that she was so wary of him. Then when he'd kissed her from behind there had been her amazing response, but that had lasted only seconds before Poppy's cries had shattered the moment and Tessa had wanted him gone.

So much for the barriers coming down. He could have nursed Poppy for her, soothed whatever it was that had brought her out of her sleep, while Tessa gave her a drink and they checked her temperature. Instead, she had wanted him gone as fast as possible and before he'd known what was what he'd found himself ejected from her home.

He'd been hoping that after tonight she might let him take her to the theatre, or out for a meal some time, or both, but clearly he'd been wrong to anticipate any such thing. She was a single parent, bringing up a child she adored, and everything else came second.

There was little chance that she would want to take time away from Poppy, and he'd been crazy to think the kiss in the kitchen had meant anything to her, other than a moment's arousing of the senses.

It had been a strange day of ups and downs. He'd been able to save the vision in one eye of a man who had looked likely to lose it completely, then he'd been invited for dinner at Tessa's—and to stay the night!

He'd actually held her in his arms for the briefest of moments until they'd come down to earth and he'd been reminded that he would never come first in Tessa's life, never be her top priority. Perhaps not be in her life at all.

The next morning she knocked on the door of the big house before going to her office in the hope of catching Drake before he left for the day, and was rewarded by the look of surprise on his face as he saw her.

'I'm sorry that you didn't manage a night away from this place,' she told him awkwardly. 'But I am always most concerned when Poppy has one of her bad dreams. She's so little and she's been through such a lot.'

'And you didn't think I might have been able to assist?' he said abruptly. 'I'm not unused to dealing with children and Poppy does know who I am.'

'I didn't ask because I was so conscious of what had been happening between us at the moment of her awakening,' she explained awkwardly, 'and it seemed inappropriate that you should stay when my position as Poppy's mother was being called into account.'

Drake looked at his watch as if time was of the essence and Tessa felt her face warming. 'Yes, I suppose so,' he said dryly. 'I'm due in Theatre in five minutes, can't stop.' And closing the door behind him, he strode off towards the hospital, leaving Tessa to interpret that as she would. The sheer male attractiveness of him once again caused heads to turn, but left her with the awful feeling that those moments in the kitchen the night before meant a lot more to her than they did to him.

Yet she'd learned one thing from them. That she wasn't as far from wanting Drake back in her life as she'd thought.

As he scrubbed up for what lay ahead in the operating theatre Drake was wishing that he hadn't been so abrupt with Tessa when she'd knocked on his door. But he'd been left with the uncomfortable sensation that for the first time in his life he wanted something very much that he couldn't have. The truth was that he had no idea what he was going to do about it.

When Tessa arrived at her office, Jennifer was already there and the first item on the agenda was an event that was to take place on the coming Saturday that the two of them were organising on behalf of the hospital management.

The picnic that had only just taken place had been basically for the children and families of staff members, while this occasion was for staff and partners only in the form of a supper dance on board a floating restaurant on a nearby river.

Tessa's involvement meant that Poppy would have to spend the night at Lizzie and Daniel's place, which they didn't mind in the least, but she, Tessa, did. Her little one had been there all week during her working hours so it didn't feel right to expect more from her friends. And no doubt Drake would be at the party looking absolutely mind-blowing, while she would be bogged down with the pressures of making sure that the organising was perfect.

When she'd invited Drake for a meal and then offered him the spare room for the night it had been because he'd had a rough day in Theatre, and she'd felt sorry for him. But it had been a major lapse of her avowal not to be alone with him except during working hours, and when Poppy had cried out she'd made a big thing of it because she'd felt guilty and ashamed for breaking her promise to herself.

What he'd thought about that she didn't know—probably decided that it was a bit over the top—but he had done as she'd asked, though his manner now was abrupt to say the least.

She and Jennifer had an appointment during the morning with the manager of the river restaurant to discuss menus and floral decorations for the event and to hand over name cards for the guests seated at each table. It was time-consuming and when they'd finished it was almost lunch-time.

On arriving back at the hospital, Tessa found a message from Drake saying that he would like to see her at four o'clock if she was free, to check on the progress of the treatment of her overactive thyroid gland.

She shuddered. It was always there, the thought

of what might happen if the medication didn't solve the problem and she had to have surgery. The only good thing about it was that at least she would have the best of his profession to perform it. But there was Poppy, small and defenceless, and she had to be able to take care of her no matter what. If Drake could give her that she could forgive him anything.

When she arrived at his consulting rooms at exactly four o'clock he was on the phone and told whoever he was speaking to that he would get back to them shortly.

It was the builder, as it happened, wanting to discuss the décor in one of the rooms in the house of his dreams and, pleasurable though it was, it came a poor second to having Tessa near for a short time, even though it was clear that there was no joy in her.

'It's early days as yet,' he said when she sat facing him across his desk, 'but I don't see any harm in checking to see if the treatment is working,'

It was true, he didn't, and after their lacklustre exchange of words at the start of the day he'd been wanting to do something to make up for his surliness.

CHAPTER SIX

So far she hadn't spoken and as he beckoned her to position herself across from him, only inches away, with her chin resting in the required position, Drake thought ironically that this was probably the nearest he was going to get to Tessa after their very brief encounter of the night before.

Once he had finished his examination he asked, 'How does your eye feel now? Does it seem any less pressured?'

'Just a little maybe,' she told him, with a feeling that what he had to say next wasn't going to be uplifting.

'Mmm,' he murmured thoughtfully. 'I can't see much improvement yet, but it is early days, Tessa, so don't be discouraged.'

'It's Poppy that I think about all the time,' she told him tearfully. 'I need to be able to take care of her, Drake. She has no one else apart from her grandfather and he is way past looking after her if I should lose my sight.'

He came round to her side and looked down at

her. 'Why don't you let *me* worry about that?' he said softly. 'I do have my uses.'

'Yes, I know,' she said. 'I'm aware of how fortunate I am to have you as my ophthalmologist.' 'But how do I know that you aren't going to move on to pastures new just when I need you?'

'I didn't leave any of my patients in the middle of treatment when I went to Switzerland. There was no one left behind to fret about my absence.'

'Except me,' she said. 'I was just a plaything for you.'

'I can't believe that you remember it as such,' he said sombrely. 'You were beautiful, divine, and I let my dream of being at the top of my profession spoil what we had.'

'Oh!' she said with surprise. 'I didn't know you saw it that way.' After a short pause she continued, 'But did you have to come back from your Swiss idyll and shatter the contentment that I'd worked so hard for?'

'That was never my intention, Tessa. I love Horizons, this place is my home, and when I was offered this position I couldn't resist coming back to where I belong.'

He glanced at a clock on the wall above their heads. 'I've got a consultation in five minutes, Tessa, but before you go will you promise me that you will trust me with your eyes?'

'Yes, of course,' she replied, and thought she would trust him with anything...except her heart.

As she was on the point of leaving he said, 'What

about the event on the river boat on Saturday. Are you going?'

She was going all right, Tessa thought. There was absolutely no way to get out of it since she and Jennifer were the organisers. Drake was waiting for an answer so she told him, 'Yes, I am. Poppy is staying at Lizzie and Daniel's.'

'So, will you save me a dance?' he wanted to know.

'I can't. I'm booked for the night.'

'What?' he exclaimed. 'You must be in big demand.'

'Yes, I am,' was the reply, and she left Drake's office overwhelmed with regret for what could have been.

When Tessa took Poppy to her friend's house on the Saturday night and Lizzie saw that she was wearing the smart navy suit that she had to wear for work she said, 'What a shame you aren't allowed to wear a dress, especially since *you know who* is going to be there.'

'It's regulatory that staff involved with organising efforts away from the hospital wear work clothes,' she told her laughingly, 'and the person in question will be too occupied with his fan club to chat to skivvies.'

After watching Poppy playing happily with the twins, Tessa went, making her way reluctantly to the riverside where the fashionable restaurant that they'd hired for the night was situated.

She hadn't seen Drake since he'd checked the progress of the eye treatment and wished herself far away from a situation where the two of them would be at the same gathering. She was apprehensive about his reaction when he discovered she was far from the belle of the ball she had presented herself as, but since she and Jennifer would be there quite some time before the guests arrived, she hoped by then to have everything under control—including herself.

It was a vain hope. They were greeted with the news that the head chef was in hospital after being knocked off his motorcycle on the way to work that evening and that the manager had gone away for the weekend. So instead of organisation there was chaos in the kitchen, with Tessa assisting the missing chef's two assistants and Jennifer doing the last-minute setting up of the dining room with the help of the bar staff.

She had taken off her jacket and was wearing a long white apron and white hat as she obeyed the orders of the two remaining chefs, and was praying that all would be ready in time. So much for being in big demand that she'd teased Drake about. She would be lucky if she even saw the dance floor.

In evening dress with a corsage of lily of the valley and pale pink roses in a florist's box on the back seat of the car, Drake had intended on arriving early to make sure he got the chance to spend some time with Tessa if possible, and as he pulled up by the riverside he smiled to see that her car was already in the restaurant's parking area.

What would she be wearing? he wondered. Whatever it was, she would look divine, and with hospital and family commitments put to one side for a few hours, maybe they could spend some time together.

When he went inside, up the gangplank's gently rocking timbers, he saw that apart from her secretary, who was chatting to a couple of bar staff, there was no one else in sight from the hospital. It was still quite early, so it wasn't surprising, but he was sure he'd seen Tessa's car parked on the river bank and was determined to catch her alone for a moment before the event kicked off.

Jennifer had seen him and when he asked where Tessa was, he was pointed in the direction of the kitchen, and in a few swift strides he was pushing back its swing doors and coming abruptly to a halt.

'What on earth!' he exclaimed, as she swung round to face him while in the process of testing a large joint of beef that looked as if it had just come out of the oven. All around her was food of one kind or another, with the kitchen staff having returned quickly to their tasks, as if his interruption was not the most pressing of demands on their attention.

Tessa was still wearing the long white apron and shapeless hat, and as it deserved an explanation she said, 'The head chef was involved in an accident on his way here and is in hospital. I was just another pair of hands, but the crisis seems to be over now.'

'Why you?' he questioned. 'Who is supposed to be in charge?'

'I am,' she informed him. 'It's part of my job.'

'So when you told me that you would be otherwise engaged when I asked you to save me a dance, it was this sort of thing that you meant?'

'I'm afraid so,' she informed him, as she took off the hat, undid the apron strings and revealed that she was wearing work clothes underneath.

He groaned as he passed her the corsage of flowers that he had hoped to see her wearing and said, 'So much for that, then.' He turned without another word and went back into the restaurant area, which was gradually filling up with hospital employees.

When the band began to play Tessa surprised him a second time by appearing beside them and their instruments—with the corsage firmly pinned to her jacket—to announce that the meal would be served in half an hour's time and there would be dancing before and after.

When Drake glanced up from reading the menu at a table at the far end of the bar he observed her, slack-jawed. She was standing before him, smiling with hand outstretched and asking, 'Can we have this dance?'

'Yes, of course,' he said, 'though what about your duties?'

'I feel that two hours over a hot stove should cover that.'

'I'm quite sure that it will,' he said laughingly, 'but aren't you forgetting something?'

'What?'

'I can't dance with you without touching you and I thought that wasn't allowed.'

'Maybe just this once,' she said, smiling back at him, and he thought how beautiful she was despite the plain navy suit bedecked with his flowers.

'So let's do it,' he said, holding out his arms, and she went into them like a nesting bird under the surprised glances of those present.

Drake was holding her close when he felt her stiffen. 'There's Daniel!' she said. 'Something must be wrong with Poppy.'

'We had better go and find out,' he said, and hand in hand they hurried towards Lizzie's husband.

'Poppy jumped off a stool with a metal whistle in her mouth and it has cut open the roof of her mouth quite badly,' he said, wasting no time. 'Lizzie and the boys are on their way to A and E with her, but needless to say it's you that she wants, Tessa. I've left my engine running so we'll soon catch them up.'

'I'm coming with you,' Drake said, and after leaving Jennifer in charge of the rest of the evening Tessa, Drake and Daniel piled into the car. Tessa was holding tightly onto him and praying that it wasn't as bad as it sounded and that Poppy wasn't afraid.

As he observed the pallor of her face and the fear of what awaited her in her eyes, Drake was debating whether parenthood was worth it, taking on a lifetime burden of care, and for someone else's child into the bargain. The enchanting Poppy had almost made him change his mind about that, but tonight was going to be the testing time.

Lizzie and the twins had arrived just before them, with Poppy crying loudly while a doctor attempted to assess the damage to the inside of her mouth, which wasn't easy under the circumstances. When he saw that Tessa had arrived he said, 'I'll leave you for a few moments while your little girl calms down and then we'll see what will be the best way to deal with the problem.'

'If you can coax her to stop crying and open her mouth while I have a look, we might be lucky and find that the injury is of such a nature that it might suction back up into position while she sleeps, as I have known it do sometimes in similar circumstances.' And off he went to see someone else who needed his attention, with a promise to be back shortly.

Since arriving, Drake had kept a low profile, standing apart from those closest to Tessa, and as she held Poppy and soothed her gently he felt that she was probably wishing him miles away right now.

They'd been sharing a precious moment of togetherness back there on the dance floor, he was thinking, but within moments the magic had gone with the news of Poppy's accident.

He supposed there was a chance that she would let *him* see inside her mouth because she knew him and so save Tessa more upset. But would she want him to try, after making it clear that she didn't want him there when Poppy had woken up from a bad dream that night? His professional instincts kicked in—the little one was hurting and he couldn't stand by and do nothing.

Tessa went weak with relief when he appeared by her side and said, 'Maybe Poppy will open wide for me. Shall I try?'

'Yes,' she said desperately, as the crying had stopped since he had appeared.

When he held out his arms Poppy went into them and gave a little whimper, but didn't cry when he said gently, 'Open your mouth wide so that I can see where it hurts.' After a gulping sort of sob she obeyed.

The doctor who'd been attending her was back and gazing in amazement at the sight of his young patient co-operating with someone he recognised as Drake Melford from his much-publicised top-ranking position at the Horizons Hospital.

'If you will take my word for it, I think you could be right about your suggestion that the roof of the mouth might suction up again when Poppy goes to sleep and is still,' he told him.

The other man nodded. 'It would save the child a lot of distress if we try that first, and to have your opinion is much appreciated.'

He turned to Tessa. 'If you are willing for that to be done, I'll phone the children's ward and make the arrangement for an overnight stay for her and we'll see what tomorrow brings.'

When he'd gone, Lizzie, who had been hovering anxiously, said, 'Thank goodness for that, Tessa. It may not be as bad as it seemed at first.' Glancing across at Drake, who was still holding Poppy, she said, 'As Dr Melford is here to give his support, we'll be off. I've got to get the boys home but I'll ring you later.'

After they'd gone he said, 'I'll carry her to the ward then I'll go, as I'm sure that you must be feeling that you've seen enough of me in the last few hours. Give me a ring in the morning when you have an answer as to whether the damaged area of Poppy's mouth has gone back into position, and I'll come and pick you up.'

Tired in both mind and body, she nodded. It had been a long, exhausting day. There had been the preparations for the event on the river boat in the morning, followed by a couple of hours in the heat of the kitchens in the afternoon, which had been quite exhausting, and then the few magic moments when they'd danced carefree and happy had been shattered by the news that her child was hurt. After that nothing else had registered, except Drake being in her life once again, and this time he had been so very welcome!

By the time they reached the ward Poppy was asleep in his arms and as he laid her down carefully on the bed that had been waiting for her, with a smiling nurse standing by, Tessa was filled with thankfulness that the first part of the nightmare was over, and if the fates were kind there might be better news in the morning.

She longed to ask Drake to stay but wasn't going

to. He had been there when she'd needed him. What more could she ask?

'You know where I'll be,' he said with a wry smile. On the point of departing, he added, 'Amongst the mothballs in the big house, but not for much longer. You may find it hard to believe but I'm in the process of buying a house and can't wait to move into it.'

If she hadn't been so tired Tessa would have wanted to know the details, but she merely nodded wearily and said, 'I hope that you will be happy in your new home.' As if it was a minor item of news amongst the other matters in her mind, she pointed to the sleeping child on the bed and said, 'If you should have any reason to speak to Randolph, please don't tell him about this.'

'Of course not,' he said dryly, with the feeling that he had been chastised for bringing mundane matters into the moment, and that much as he wanted to stay he needed to relieve Tessa of his presence and let her sleep. So, with a last glance at Poppy, he went.

The night staff had found her a comfortable chair beside the bed and every so often came to check on their young patient, and in the meantime, as the hours dawdled by, Tessa was able to take in the surprising news of Drake's about-turn on his views of the time they'd spent together.

She had changed her ideas long ago—the no-babies-no-mortgages idea was long gone. All right, it was someone else's child that she loved, and her home was a small cottage, yet it all felt so right, and until Drake had come back to unsettle her she'd been content.

The moments she'd spent in his arms on the dance floor of the river boat had been exactly how she'd known they would be. They'd brought memories of that other time back in full force, and if it hadn't been for Poppy's accident she would have given in to them.

At the worst possible moment Drake had told her that he of all people had bought a house and now in the quiet night her mind was adjusting to the news. Now she was filled with questions—where? What? How…? But most of all, why? When she saw him again she hoped to get some answers.

Maybe he'd taken the step because he loved Glenminster and the villages dotted around it that were a source of delight. If the house he was buying was local, the very fact of what he was contemplating had to mean that his wanderings were over, and she didn't know how she would feel about that. Would she be able to cope with Drake at Horizons for the rest of their lives?

Poppy stirred in her sleep, gave a little moan, then opened her eyes and said croakily, 'Drink, Mummy Two.'

The nurses had left some water by her bed and when Tessa raised her up against the pillows Poppy drank thirstily, looked around her and said, 'I'm hungry.'

One of the nurses had appeared and she said,

'Not until the doctor has had a look at the inside of her mouth, I'm afraid, but she can have plenty of liquids.'

Drake was deep in thought. While Daniel had been driving them to Accident and Emergency he had told himself that tonight he would finally know what he wanted in his life, and he did.

He'd tried to stay on the edge of things and let Tessa, her friends and the doctor in charge deal with what had happened to Poppy. But he loved the child too much to stand by when she was hurt, and by taking over had admitted to himself how much she meant to him.

As for Tessa, he wanted her back in his life completely, but he knew she had doubts about how she felt about him, and like a crazy fool he'd told her about the house he was buying at the worst possible moment. Naturally she hadn't been in the least interested, with her little girl hurt and crying. He had made a proper mess of the whole thing.

When he rang the hospital in the quiet of a bright Sunday morning, ready to set off immediately if the news was good, he wasn't disappointed, at least not right away.

Tessa's voice had a lift to it as she told him that Poppy had slept through the night and what they had hoped for had happened, the roof of her mouth had suctioned back into place and the doctors there were allowing her to be discharged with an instruction that for the next few days she have only soft foods and liquids.

'Fantastic!' he cried. 'I'll come and get you.'

'There's no need,' she told him. 'I've got a taxi waiting outside, but thanks for the offer, Drake.'

'All right.' It was an effort to sound casual but he felt her rejection to his core. Tessa was clearly on her guard again.

Surely he didn't think that what had happened the night before was going to bring them back to how they used to be? Tessa thought. It would always be there, the magnetism they had for each other, but she'd lived without it for three years…no, it was nearly four, and she had no intention of altering the arrangement.

As they walked slowly towards the waiting taxi Poppy was looking around her and Tessa didn't have to question who it was she sought. Knowing that Drake had been there the night before, she would be wanting to know where he was now.

The answer to that was he'd gone to seek comfort in the only place where he could find it. In one of the villages up in the hills was the house where he'd been hoping to bring Tessa and Poppy one day.

It was only during the long night that the thought had become a certainty in his mind, and it had taken just one short sentence when she'd rebuffed him to wipe it clear.

* * *

The builder was on the job when he got there, at the top of a ladder, putting some finishing touches to the house, and Drake thought that whatever else he might have got wrong this was not it. His job at the Horizons Hospital wouldn't leave him much time for leisure, but however much it did he would spend it here in this beautiful house...lonely as hell.

'You don't look too happy,' the man said. 'Is it something to do with this place?'

'No, not at all, it's fabulous,' he told him. 'How long will it be before it's finished?'

'Three weeks, a month at the most.'

'So I'll soon be free of the mothballs.'

'I can guarantee that,' the builder promised laughingly. 'So why don't I take you for another tour of your new home, show you the progress?'

On the way home in the taxi Tessa felt like weeping. His casual acceptance of her decision to take a taxi hurt. She sighed at how foolish she was being. Was she so afraid that he would shatter her contentment? Could she not let him in just a little?

Were its foundations so feeble that she couldn't let him share in the joy of discovering that Poppy's accident had proved not so serious as they'd at first thought? Some of it had been due to him because her small daughter liked him, trusted him—which was getting to be a problem—and it was that thought that had prompted her to phone for a taxi, and which was why she was now on the way home with Poppy cuddled up close, asking where Drake was.

To add to Tessa's unease there was the moment when he'd told her about the house he was buying, and now that Poppy was fine she was burning with curiosity about where it was, when he would be moving in, what it was like—and, of course, what had prompted him to buy it.

It was Sunday once more. No chance of seeing Drake again until Monday morning at the clinic to try to make amends for her rudeness after everything he had done for her and her family, and Tessa resigned herself to a day of keeping watch over Poppy's intake of light foods and liquids, even managing to coax her to have a sleep in the afternoon.

It was evening after what had been a long day. Poppy was asleep up above when a car she didn't recognise pulled up outside the cottage with Drake behind the wheel.

With her heartbeat quickening, Tessa watched as he uncoiled himself from the driving seat and walked slowly up to the door. When she opened it to him he said quizzically, 'I waited until I was sure that Poppy would be asleep before coming, as I didn't want to be any more intrusive than I was yesterday.'

As she stepped back to let him in she swallowed hard. Drake had been there when she'd needed him and was describing it as an intrusion. She wanted to throw herself into his arms, let him back into her life totally, but couldn't because he was saying breezily,

'I got your point about the taxi, so spent the afternoon with the builder at the house I'm buying and then went to the garage to pick up the car that you see at the bottom of your drive.

'It has been on order for a few weeks and they phoned yesterday to say that it had arrived, so today I got the chance to do both of those very pleasing things.'

'Yes, I see,' she said stiffly. 'I'm sorry I didn't get the chance to ask about your decision to become a homeowner. I suppose it's because you are so weary of your present accommodation?'

'Partly, but not entirely,' he replied. 'It is more that I fell in love with it and had to have it. You may recall that I am rather inclined to be like that. But, in general, I'm learning to hold onto precious things, am changing some of my views on life.'

'And so where is it, this house that you've fallen in love with?' she asked, without taking him up on that last comment.

'In one of the villages. It will be ready soon and I shall commute daily to the hospital, but I didn't come to discuss that. I'm here to ask about Poppy's mouth. Any problems?'

'No,' she said flatly. 'It seems all right. We've had a quiet day, unlike your own, and I will be at my desk as usual tomorrow.'

'Fine, but the place won't fall apart without you.

Why not take another day to get over the weekend's traumas?'

'I'm aware that my position at Horizons is much less important than yours,' she told him wryly, 'but I'm a working mother and take my responsibilities seriously.'

'I do know that, and I admire you for it,' he said easily, 'but there must be times when you need a helping hand. You have only to ask. And now that I know that Poppy is all right I'll be off.' And before she could think of something to say that would delay his departure, he went striding back to his new car with the sheer male charisma of him turning her bones to jelly and her heart to lead.

Upstairs Poppy whimpered in her sleep and as she hurried to her Tessa was aware of the irony of the situation she found herself in. Poppy already loved Drake and would be happy to have his presence always there, but her own love for him was a battered and bruised thing that was reluctant to be brought back to life. The only cure for that was to avoid him as much as possible, but that strategy could hardly be any worse!

And as if a prod in that direction the voice of conscience was there to remind her that he wasn't the one who hadn't kept to the vows they'd made. She had been that person, and as the last rays of the sun slanted across the hilltops like the bands of gold of that other time, the memory hurt now just as much as it had then.

CHAPTER SEVEN

THE NEXT MORNING Tessa was treating it as back to normal, with herself at the hospital and Poppy at Lizzie's for the day. She would have liked to inspect the inside of Poppy's mouth before she left her, just to be sure that all was well, but was getting no co-operation as the light breakfast she'd made for her was of more interest than obeying the request to 'open wide'.

Just as she was about to give up the phone rang and Drake's voice came over the line. 'Would you like me to call round to check Poppy's mouth before you take her to your friends?' he asked. 'Or have you already accomplished that?'

She almost groaned. Here he was again, her daughter's favourite person. It went without saying that Poppy would oblige for him.

'No. I haven't,' she admitted, 'but not for want of trying. I would be grateful if you would come, Drake, as I'm concerned that there might be some damage that isn't obvious.'

'How long before you leave for your childminder's?'

'Forty-five minutes.'

'I'll be round before then.' So much for avoiding him.

But she couldn't fault Drake's concern for her child, even though he was continually turning *her* world upside down.

'Looks fine,' he said after Poppy had opened her mouth to its widest for him. 'I'll drop her off at your friend's house, if you like, to save you the journey into town after the harrowing weekend you've had.'

'It's kind of you to offer,' she told him, 'but, no, thanks, we'll be fine. I have a suggestion of my own, though, that I'd like to put to *you*.'

He was smiling, unabashed. 'Let me guess. Could it be a request that I stop interfering in your life?'

'No, it isn't. It is connected with you having some breakfast while you're here because I'm sure that coming to check Poppy's mouth means that you haven't had time to eat.'

'It's a tempting thought, but I ought to be off,' he protested weakly. 'I really haven't the time to wait while you prepare me a meal, Tessa.'

'It's ready,' she informed him calmly. 'I cooked bacon and eggs while we were waiting for you to come, and tea and toast will only take a matter of minutes, so take a seat.'

'Why?' he asked, obeying the request. 'Why are

you doing this when you've made it clear you don't want me in your life?'

She was placing the food in front of him and said, 'I don't know. I must be crazy, but I do owe you an apology for the way I behaved about the taxi. It got shelved when I heard what a lovely day you'd had.'

'Yes, it was a riot,' he said dryly, with the memory of gazing at the house he was buying and thinking again that he was going to be as lonely as hell in it.

When he'd finished eating Drake said, 'I need to see how the medication you are on for the eye problem is progressing. When are you free?'

She shuddered. The mere mention of it made her feel nervous, but he was waiting for an answer and she told him, 'Not today if you don't mind. I left my secretary to clear away after the event on the river boat and feel that I must be available to sort out any loose ends that I may have left before anything else. Would tomorrow be all right?'

'Sure,' he said easily. 'I'll give you a buzz when I've sorted out a suitable time. And, Tessa, don't feel so apprehensive at the thought. It's a trifle early for results, but we'll see... And now I must go, I've a busy day ahead of me.'

He longed to hold her close again, if only for a moment. It had been magical having her in his arms as they'd danced on Saturday night, but it had been short-lived and he wasn't going to risk a rebuff at this hour of the day. The new Tessa could be unpredictable and he needed a clear head to get through what looked to be a very busy day.

So, bending to pat Poppy's dark locks as she came to stand beside him, he smiled across at her and said, 'Thanks for the breakfast. It was a lifesaver.' And when seconds later his car pulled away Tessa felt as if the day had lost its meaning.

Drake's face was set in sombre lines as he drove the short distance to the hospital. A quick glance while at the cottage hadn't shown any big improvement in Tessa's eye, but he needed her where his equipment was to decide about that. He understood her anxiety about caring for Poppy and maybe underneath was the dread that he might muscle into their lives if she couldn't cope for any reason.

She had softened towards him, though not to the degree that she wanted him back as before. So it was going to be a case of treading carefully and doing all he could to allay her fears. Being too pushy wasn't the answer. He had to face up to the fact that the future still held a lot of questions.

Horizons had just come into sight, the old stone building that had once been a wool mill and was now used for a far worthier purpose. As Drake glanced at the hills above the thought came, Would Tessa ever want him again, need him like he was beginning to need her, and want to live in that lovely house with him?

With that thought uppermost he parked the car and the day closed in on him, with a clinic in the morning, Theatre in the afternoon and a special appointment for Randolph in the evening to discuss his next cataract surgery, which was coming up soon.

He liked the old guy and when the consultation was over said, 'Can I ask you something personal?'

'Sure, go ahead,' was the reply, because Drake was liked in return.

'Do I resemble Poppy's father in any way?'

'Yes, you do,' Randolph told him without hesitation. 'The dark hair and hazel eyes, the bone structure of your face and your height. I think Poppy is confused—sometimes she seems to think you *are* him, but then she doesn't understand why you and Tessa are so at odds. The two of you don't get on, do you?'

'We had an affair before I went to Switzerland to take up a promotion, and I hurt her a lot by behaving like an idiot and leaving her behind.'

'Ah! So that's it,' Randolph said. 'I did wonder. So are you going to do anything about it?'

Drake's smile was wry. 'I'm working on it.'

If he hadn't promised Tessa that he wouldn't mention her eye problem to Poppy's grandfather he would have told him that the unromantic but vital task of sorting out her vision had to come before anything else, and that he was hoping that tomorrow might have some answers for both of them.

Yet it *was* still early days to expect significant improvement in her eye. First the treatment had to disperse an accumulation of debris behind the eye that had built up over recent weeks before being seen to have any effect. Only time would tell if surgery was required.

When he saw her the following day she looked pale and tense and greeted him with the news that her Aunt Sophie, the younger sister of her mother, who had died when she'd been in her late teens, had phoned for a chat, and on discovering that she had an eye problem had said that she'd once had something similar and so had her mother, that it ran in their family.

As he listened to what she had to say Drake wanted to reach out to her, hold her close, and tell her that he would always be there for her, but Tessa's expression was indicating that it was strictly a doctor-patient moment, and she was hardly likely to believe him anyway, with his track record of disappearing when the mood took him.

'Yes, hyperthyroidism can be hereditary,' he agreed, 'but so are quite a few other illnesses and the medication for this one can take a while to clock in, so shall we see what it's been up to?'

When he'd finished checking the eye from all angles and had measured what was a minor reduction of the problem with the orbital area of her eye he said gently, 'We have a small success. Does your eye feel more comfortable at all?'

'Yes, a little,' she told him, and smiled for the first time since appearing before him. 'I've been reading up on these kinds of conditions and they can be quite scary, so thank you for being here for me, Drake.'

'Thanks aren't necessary,' he said, smiling across at her, and took advantage of the moment. 'How about you let me take you for a meal to celebrate the slight though most welcome improvement? To somewhere more upmarket than my previous suggestion of the staff restaurant in this place.'

There was silence for a moment of the kind indicating that the other person intended to be firm but polite. 'I'm sorry,' she said. 'I can't ask Lizzie to have Poppy more than she does already, and don't you think the two of us see enough of each other already? From a distance, maybe, which seems the most sensible arrangement, but nevertheless...'

'Oh, by all means let's keep our distance!' he said tightly. 'All I am doing is asking you out to lunch, Tessa.'

She swallowed hard. Didn't he see that her unwillingness to dine with him and take their frail relationship a step further was because of her dread that he might do the same thing again if the mood took him? Leave her behind? Which now would hurt Poppy as well as herself, and she couldn't bear the thought of that happening.

But to reject what on the face of it was just an invitation to take her for a meal had the sound of playing hard to get over something of minor importance. Finally she caved in and said, 'Yes, all right about the meal, but in the daytime during Monday to Friday so that I don't put any extra pressure on Lizzie.'

He nodded. 'All right, I'll take a couple of hours off around midday tomorrow, as long as you're able to do the same. We'll drive into the town to a smart restaurant somewhere. And now, if you'll excuse me, I have work to do.'

'Yes, of course,' she said weakly, and went back to where Jennifer observed her curiously.

In spite of her reluctance to socialise alone with Drake, the next morning Tessa had an insane longing to dress up for him, because apart from on the odd occasion he hadn't seen her in anything but her office clothes since he'd come back into her life, and putting the dark blue jacket and skirt to one side she surveyed the clothes in her wardrobe.

Gone were the days when she had revelled in making herself look beautiful for him with smart clothes and jewellery. A turquoise dress of fine linen caught her eye, mainly because he had always loved to see her in it.

If she wore it today it would have another message, one that told him she wasn't just the single mother of a small child having to work to survive, but a beautiful woman, just as he was a man who had heads turning wherever he went. If he ever asked if she had forgiven him for walking out of her life so uncaringly, she was beginning to feel that she could truthfully say that she had, but that was as far as it went.

Yet it didn't stop her from being afraid that he might come knocking on her door early one morning like that other time, and with her melting in his arms carry her upstairs… But this time she wouldn't be alone. Poppy would be there, sleeping in her pretty little room, and he would never do anything to upset the child who sometimes thought he was her father.

In the end she chose not to wear the turquoise dress. If Drake got the wrong signal it could be harder than ever to stop him from thinking it was just a matter of time before she melted into his arms again. So it was a top of apricot silk, slim-line cream trousers and high-heeled shoes that she arrived in at the office, to Jennifer's amazement.

'What's going on?' the other woman asked laughingly. 'Are you going out straight from here tonight?'

'No,' was the reply. 'Drake Melford is taking me out to lunch. I have an eye problem that is worrying me and he wants to discuss it in more relaxing surroundings than these. It will be just a matter of taking an extended lunch break, and the clothes are…er…'

'To let him see how beautiful you are out of the clothes that we spend our working days in?' Jennifer teased. 'Because when he sees you it's going to knock him out cold.'

Better cold than hot, Tessa thought wryly, so why was she doing this?

There was no sign of Drake during the morning, just a brief phone call to say he would be waiting in the car park at half past eleven, if that was all right. When she'd assured him that it was he'd rung off, and now it was just five minutes to go, and she was making her way there, wishing she'd worn her usual work clothes instead of dressing up like a Christmas tree.

He followed her outside seconds later and when he saw her his eyes widened. As far as he was concerned, the occasion came from a longing to be with her, even for just a short time, disguised as a working lunch in the middle of a busy day. The last thing he'd expected had been that Tessa would have dressed up for it. Was it a sign of forgiveness, temptation or a moment of mockery? He wished he knew, but it was as if the sun up above was shining just on them and maybe the hurts of the past would be forgotten for a while.

'It's nice to see you out of your usual work clothes for once,' he said casually and left it at that as they drove out of the hospital grounds, having no wish to say the wrong thing in the moment of meeting.

'It's good to have a change sometimes,' she said in a similar tone, and with a glance at what he was wearing thought that no one could fault Drake's appearance. His suit had the style and quality that he always kept to.

'I've booked a table at the new hotel in the gardens at the end of the shopping promenade,' he said, as the town came in sight, and thought Tessa couldn't fault that for tact. No going to one of their old haunts to pull at her heartstrings. They were too far apart for that sort of thing.

'So how is little Poppy?' he asked, when they

had been shown to a table in the restaurant. 'Is her mouth still all right?'

She smiled. 'Yes, thank goodness.'

He nodded. 'It was fortunate that it was the roof of the mouth, which in such cases can suck back upwards easily, instead of the bottom of the mouth, where injuries can be more serious.'

With a change of subject he went on to say, 'When Randolph came for an appointment the other day I asked him outright if I resembled her father in any way. He said yes and was quite definite about it. So, Tessa, I do hope you don't still think I'm using Poppy's attraction to me to ease myself into your life again.'

As their glances locked she said, 'I did, but I don't any more, Drake. It's just a most unusual co-incidence and if it makes Poppy happy, it's all right with me.'

'Just as long as I don't want to take it to its natural conclusion,' he commented dryly.

'Yes, you could say that. She has already had one father who through no fault of his own disappeared out of her life, another would be just too much for her young mind if you decided to move on again to pastures new."

There'd been nothing green about his time in Switzerland, he thought grimly. It had been cold outside and he'd been cold inside with the misery that had always been there when he thought about how in his arrogance he'd left behind the special woman in his life.

But this getting together for a meal was supposed to help put Tessa's mind at rest as much as possible about the thyroid over-activity that was affecting her eye.

Blood tests were showing a slight improvement in the condition, but there was some way to go before he would be able to tell her anything definite. An under active thyroid was easier to deal with by far than one that was the opposite.

He could remember some years ago having to remove the four parathyroids from an elderly woman's neck because they were overworking and causing her calcium levels to rise dangerously, making such things as benign tumours appear, and causing serious kidney defects along with other life threatening illnesses, and it could have been the same with Tessa's problem.

So far there had been none of the hazards associated with the problem except for the eye protruding from the socket and there had been a very small sign of improvement the last time he'd done a blood test but there was a way to go before the problem was sorted.

So he didn't let himself be drawn about her lack of faith regarding his reliability and said, 'The medication is beginning to work and now we might see a reduction in the pressure around the optic nerve and your eye feeling more comfortable. Then it really will be time to celebrate.'

The food had arrived, it was time to eat, and they

talked about minor things until she said, 'So where exactly is the house that you're buying, Drake?'

'Why don't you let me take you to see it instead of talking about it?'

She didn't reply to that, instead asked casually, as if she wasn't bothered one way or the other, 'Are you intending living there alone or will someone be sharing it with you?'

'A couple of folks might if I can persuade them, but it will be a few weeks before it is ready for occupation,' he explained, 'and then it will be goodbye to where I'm living now, thank goodness. Would you feel like giving some advice when it comes to furnishings?'

She was observing him, startled. 'Er, yes, I suppose so, but I don't really want to be involved in something that might be wrong for others.'

He was smiling across at her and she thought he was still the most attractive man she had ever met. It wasn't surprising that from the first moment of their meeting she'd adored him and that it was taking all her willpower not to let it happen again.

The moments on the dance floor, the time when he'd kissed her in the rose garden and the brief moments of desire they'd shared in her kitchen were like an oasis in a dry land. But there was the new life she'd made for herself and Poppy with its special kind of contentment that she couldn't risk.

'It's what I like that counts, anyone else doesn't matter,' he was saying, safe in the knowledge that if they ever did have a fresh start and she and Poppy lived with him in his house up on the hillside he would be sure to like the furnishings because she would have chosen them, and if that wasn't reaching for the moon he didn't know what was.

They'd finished the meal and the clock in the restaurant said there was a short time left before they had to return to the hospital, so Drake suggested a walk in the hotel gardens and said, 'When I passed a couple of days ago there was a wedding taking place and I thought what a beautiful setting it is.'

'Yes, all right,' she agreed reluctantly, having no wish to be reminded of such things while they were together, and was amazed that he who had scorned matrimony had commented on it so favourably.

There was his obvious love of Poppy, he was buying a house, and now Drake was speaking admiringly about a wedding he'd seen. Could this be the same man who had left her all those years ago?

The gardens *were* lovely, the moments together in them filled with promise, but a promise of what? she questioned. Their time had been and gone long ago. She had branched off into a different kind of life since then, separate and fulfilling. Did she want to change?

This isn't working Drake thought, casting a sideways glance at her expression. If you are going to woo Tessa you have to come up with something better than this. Why don't you ask her to marry you outright?

The words were forming themselves in his mind,

but on the point of saying them he saw that in
Tessa's expression there was nothing but the wish
to get back to the hospital and reality. It wasn't the
right moment, he decided, far from it, and led the
way to where he'd parked the car, unable to ignore
the relief in her expression.

He was expecting a speedy departure from her when
they arrived back at the hospital, but instead Tessa
turned to face him in the confines of the car and
said, 'I'd like to return your hospitality. When would
it be convenient for you to come for dinner with
Poppy and me at the cottage?'

He was observing her sombrely. 'You don't have
to do that because I took you out to lunch. If you remember, it was to celebrate that the over-functioning
of your thyroid gland was beginning to slow down.
So don't feel that you have to invite me back.'

'You don't want to see Poppy, then?'

'Of course I want to see her, but not on suffer-
ance!'

'What makes you say that?' she protested.

Drake, the memory of his aborted marriage proposal still fresh in his head, had his answer ready.
'It might be because you were so obviously bored
back there.'

'If that is what you really think you are so wrong,'
she told him. 'I feel as if I don't know you any more.
Your thinking is different. All the things that you
didn't want as part of your life then are acceptable
to you now.'

'And is that not allowed?' he asked.

'No, of course it is, but my life was sorted long ago. As I picked up the pieces of what I'd thought was a love that would last for ever I discovered that there was a lot less pain in loving a child than loving a man.'

'So you intend to stay as you are, just you and Poppy in your safe little cocoon?'

Tessa didn't answer. Her glance was on the clock on the front of the hospital building and she said hastily, 'I have a new food supplier arriving in ten minutes, Drake, I must go.'

'Yes, me too,' he agreed. 'I have a cataract removal this afternoon.'

'I do hope it goes well,' she said softly. 'That is so much more important than what I will be doing.'

'You know our patients need nourishment as well as eyesight, and Tessa, I'd like to accept your dinner invitation, if it still stands.'

She smiled. 'Yes, of course it does. I thought of lunch during the weekend so that you will have more time to be with Poppy than in the evening. Which day would suit you best?'

'Sunday would be fine if that if that is all right with you. I usually work on Saturdays.' On that promise they went their separate ways into Horizons, with their own skylines looking momentarily brighter.

When Drake arrived on the Sunday morning Poppy was on the drive, playing on a small scooter that was her latest treasure, and as his car stopped outside the gate she became still until she saw who was in it and then as he eased himself out and came towards her she began to run towards him, and as he swung her up into his arms the name was on her lips for the first time… 'Daddy!'

For Tessa, who was following close behind, it was the moment of truth. As their glances met above Poppy's dark curls the quiet contentment she had so treasured with just the two of them was disappearing. She would have to talk to Poppy about it once Drake had gone, to help clear up what must be a very confusing situation for her little girl.

Drake's smile was rueful as he placed Poppy back onto her scooter and when she'd gone whizzing off he said, 'I told you what Randolph said about the likeness, but I didn't tell you that I asked him if the poor guy would be upset if he knew that his little girl thought another man was him and he said, no, not at all, that somewhere in the ether his daughter and son-in-law would want what would make their little girl happiest. That her father, who'd been a great guy, wouldn't mind someone else taking his place if it brought comfort.'

She looked white and withdrawn, as if a cold hand was squeezing her heart. It would be so easy to give in and let Drake back into her life for Poppy's sake, but that wouldn't do. She had made a good life for the two of them out of sadness and hurt, and it hadn't always been easy with the memory of what it was like to be in Drake's arms, in Drake's bed, the kind of things that were only ever going to happen again in her dreams.

'I want us to carry on as we are doing,' she said, 'with you living in your lovely new house and Poppy and me in our home. You can see her whenever you want, but you know that it works both ways, Drake. She has to be able to see you when she needs you— you have to be there for her too.'

It was a hurtful thing to say, and she wished she could take it back the moment she'd said it. His glance was cold as he told her, 'I know how it works, Tessa. You and I had an agreement—you can't hold that against me for ever.'

Yes, but I do, Tessa thought raggedly. Can't Drake see that? I've had the foundations of my life crumble once. I couldn't face it again. But he is so confident, so keen to make sure I remember that I wasn't entirely blameless all that time ago. Should I try a second time round?

She had cooked foods that she knew he liked and watching his enjoyment of them brought back memories of the two of them arriving home from their different workplaces and while the food was cooking making love wherever the mood took them.

They had been days of reckless rapture and even more reckless promises about the lives they intended to live devoid of responsibilities. But all that had come to Drake living alone in a rented house in the hospital grounds and her a single mother with a child that wasn't his.

He was reading her mind and when the three of them had finished eating he said, 'Let's fill the dishwasher and go out into the garden for some playtime with Poppy. I see no reason why she should suffer for our lack of rapport.'

'Yes, you're right,' she agreed, holding back tears at the thought of such a farce. What Randolph had said about Poppy's father made her feel trapped. Nothing was clear and uncomplicated any more, and after Drake left in the early evening and Poppy was asleep, Tessa watched the sun go down and tried not to think about times past.

CHAPTER EIGHT

WHETHER IT WAS because of that she didn't know, but in the stillness of the night she dreamt that she was in Drake's arms and it was magical. Consequently, when she awoke the next morning she felt tired and low-spirited.

Lizzie didn't miss her lacklustre appearance when she dropped Poppy off, and wanted to know how Sunday lunch had gone. Tessa could only manage to give a silent thumbs-down as she departed to face Monday morning at the hospital.

After the trauma of Sunday she was hoping that Drake would stay out of her radius and wasn't happy to find him perched on the corner of her desk chatting to Jennifer, when she arrived.

'Hi, there,' he said in greeting. 'Just stopped by to leave you an appointment card for next week. Now that the treatment is working I need to see you more often.'

The phone rang, her secretary answered it, and while she was taking the call he said in a low voice, 'We need to talk. When can I see you alone?'

'I don't know. I'd rather not,' she told him.

He frowned. 'I'm getting a little tired of being cast as the archvillain in your life.'

'Lunchtime, then, at the big house?' she suggested reluctantly, and he nodded and went on his way, leaving her wishing that she hadn't been so obliging in agreeing to his demands. But wasn't that how she'd always been?

When she rang the bell Drake greeted her unsmilingly and invited her to take a seat in its huge sitting room. She obeyed with the feeling that what he had to say was unlikely to be good, and waited to hear what he had to say.

It was brief, to the point, and incredible.

'When I got home from your place last night there was a message waiting for me from a clinic in Canada, offering me a similar position to the one I have here, and I've arranged to go over there in a couple of weeks' time to see what's on offer.'

He was about to take temptation out of her way, and relief was washing over her, but only for seconds until reality took over. 'You can't leave us now!' she said in a strangulated whisper. 'Poppy doesn't want a father figure who is there one moment and gone the next. She has had enough hurts in her young life.'

He didn't reply to that, just commented, 'I notice that there's no concern at the thought of my departure with regard to yourself?'

'I don't care about myself,' she cried. 'You've already messed my life up by coming back, but she's so small and defenceless.'

Tears, warm and stinging, were forming behind closed eyelids as she tried to shut him out of her vision, because Poppy wasn't the only one who was defenceless when it came to Drake. So far she'd been able to cope with his return and the effect it was having on her life but not any more.

She'd already had to pick up the pieces after one of his departures, had she the strength to do it again, this time with a child to think of?

'I'm only considering the Canadian offer because you've made it clear you don't want me here,' he said, 'and Poppy will soon forget me once I've gone. If you marry at some time in the future she will have an adoptive father to go with an adoptive mother and all will be well.'

'I can't believe that you could be so smug about something so important,' she said, fighting to maintain her self-control. 'Is that it, you have nothing more to hit me with?'

'That's it,' he said levelly. 'I didn't plan it. The offer came out of the blue at what seemed to be just the right moment in both our lives.'

'Yours maybe,' she told him, 'not mine and Poppy's. Apart from anything else, you promised to be there for me with regard to treating my eye problem. What are you going to do about that, shuffle me on to whoever takes your place?'

'I'll sort something, don't worry. If I take this

offer I won't be living on the moon. There *are* air-lines, you know.'

'Don't come back out of limbo again for my sake,' she told him flatly. 'What about the house that you're buying?'

'I shall still buy it and use it for holidays if I accept the offer. Or rent it out.'

Tessa was on her feet, holding onto the arms of the chair as she asked, 'And is that it? No other me, me, me kind of news you have to pass on?'

Drake shook his head wearily. 'No, nothing else. But, Tessa, you can't have it both ways. You don't want me around, but you don't like it when I'm prepared to oblige and get out of your life.'

The door was wide open, flung back on its hinges, and she had gone. As he closed it slowly behind her the room felt cold, as cold as it had been in Switzerland.

The rest of the day dragged on. She forced herself to concentrate on hospital matters with Jennifer's chatter in the background about what a lovely weekend she'd had with her new man friend, and all the time Tessa was imagining the pain of yet another separation from Drake. He was treating it as if she was to blame—maybe she was.

He'd been nothing but kind and caring and supportive since coming back into her life, and what had she been? Mistrusting? Unpleasant? It wasn't surprising that he was ready once again to go his own way, and ahead of them was an uncomfortable fortnight until he flew to Canada to investigate what was on offer for him out there, which was certain to be spectacular. It would need to be to lure him away from Horizons.

When she arrived at Lizzie's house after a dreadful day her friend's first words were, 'You look ghastly. What's happened?'

'Drake has been headhunted by a hospital in Canada and is going to see what's on offer in a couple of weeks, and it's all my fault, Lizzie. He's tired of me keeping him at arm's length and being so mistrusting and...well, I have to admit, sometimes I've been rude and hurtful—when that other time was just as much my fault as his.

'Poppy called him Daddy yesterday, which was fine by me until we got our wires crossed as usual and ended up putting on a big pretence of playing in the garden with her. Then he went, with things as bad as they've ever been between us, and as if the fates were weary of our lack of trust in each other the Canadian offer was waiting for him when he arrived back at the big house.'

Lizzie was observing her sadly. 'Tessa, when are you going to admit that you still love him?'

'Why not ask me when I'm going to climb Everest or something equally difficult? Why couldn't he be any man instead of Drake Melford? He loves Horizons and I'm driving him away from the place. The only way that I can admit to myself that I still love him is to do something that will make him stay.'

'And what might that be?'

'Move out of the area. Give him the space that he deserves without judging him all the time. Then he can carry on with his plans to buy a house in one of the villages and live there in contentment.'

'You can't do that!' Lizzie exclaimed in horror.

'I can. Before Drake leaves on his visit to Canada I shall tell him that if he proceeds with his crazy plan of moving there to be away from me, he will find me gone when he comes back to say his good-byes to the folks at Horizons.

'The hospital needs him, Lizzie, and if I can't persuade him to change his mind I will appeal to his conscience by having left when he comes back after looking the Canadian place over. Once he is airborne I shall put the cottage up for sale and find somewhere not too far away to move to, and once that has been sorted Poppy and I will go into temporary accommodation until the sale goes through.'

'Where have you got in mind?' Lizzie asked un-believingly.

'Maybe Devon, or somewhere not quite so far away, so that I can visit you regularly and keep an eye on Randolph, and once I've found somewhere to live please don't tell anyone except Daniel where I am, will you?'

'Of course I won't,' she assured her, staggered at the scenario that was unfolding before her. 'We shall miss the two of you so much,' she told her sadly.

'Please don't make it any harder,' Tessa begged, with her glance on Poppy playing happily in the garden with the twins.

Driving past the park on their way home, she brought the car to a halt. Workmen were delivering new benches and putting the old ones into a truck. The one that had such sweet and sour memories was the next one to go.

'Can I buy it?' she asked, pointing to the bench in question.

'Yes,' she was told. 'Unwanted things such as these are sold and the money goes to charities. This lot are fifty pounds each, including delivery.'

'You have a deal,' she told them. 'I live on the road that goes past the eye hospital.'

'Right, we'll drop it off now if you like,' one of them said, and with a sick feeling that both she and the bench were surplus to requirements she led the way.

'Where do you want it?' he asked, when they arrived at the cottage. 'On the patio at the back, please,' Tessa told him, having no wish for Drake to see it if he should happen to drive past. When they'd gone she stood observing it in silence as Poppy whizzed to and fro on her scooter.

It was a strange thing to choose as a memento of a dead love affair, she thought, but if every time she sat on the bench it brought Drake near in her self-imposed exile, it might take some of the hurt away.

Randolph rang in the late evening. It seemed that Drake had told him about his proposed Canadian trip and he wanted to know what if anything was going on between them.

'Nothing is going on,' she told him uncomfortably. 'He has the chance of a fantastic opportunity over there and is flying across to see what is on offer.'

'Surely you don't want him to leave you and Poppy back here while he goes to live and work in another country?' he questioned.

'It has happened to me before, Randolph, and what Drake does is his own affair. We have no claim on him.'

'No, of course not,' he agreed vaguely, and rang off, leaving Tessa with another problem to worry about. Randolph wasn't going to want to be far away from his granddaughter.

After Monday's day of despair Drake rang her office the next morning and said in clipped tones that he would want to check her eye once each week before he left on his Canadian trip, so how about on the mornings of the two Fridays before he flew out in the afternoon of the second one?

'Er, yes,' she agreed, remembering how she'd accused him of leaving her in the middle of the treatment if he took a job abroad.

'So shall we say first thing on each Friday?' he suggested. 'I'm going to be pushed to get all my commitments here dealt with before I leave.'

'How long do you expect to be away?' she asked, as if only mildly interested, when, in fact, she was aching for him to stay.

'I have no idea, but does it matter?' he questioned. 'You aren't going to miss me.'

She didn't reply to that. Just rang off and sat gazing through the window to where the hills that they both loved so much and the gracious town nestling beneath them seemed to be saying, If you can persuade Drake to refuse the Canadian offer and stay here, you won't have loved in vain.

She rang him back a few moments later and said, 'You shouldn't leave Horizons because of me. The hospital needs you, Glenminster needs you. So I've decided to leave the hospital and the area in order to give you some space. Perhaps you could keep that in mind while you're being shown around the Canadian set-up.' Tessa rang off before he could comment. *Coward*, she thought.

But he rang back only minutes later and said, 'I'm free for a short time and am hoping that it will be long enough to tell you what I think about your ridiculous idea, Tessa. I am quite capable of sorting out my affairs without you offering yourself as a sacrificial lamb. Don't even think of taking Poppy to some strange place because of me!

'I made a mistake coming back and I'm going to rectify it. It's as simple as that, and I'm expecting that by the time you come for your appointment on Friday you will have seen sense.' Drake put the phone down without knowing that she was going to proceed to Plan B regardless.

It was a week of miserable activity: putting the cottage up for sale without a 'for sale' sign until he had flown to Canada on the second Friday, searching for a place to move to that would meet her needs and Poppy's, somewhere that was not too near and not too far, and when she'd found the right sort of place—if ever there could be such a thing without Drake—starting afresh with little enthusiasm.

She'd spoken to the chairman and explained that she might have to leave without the usual month's notice. He'd been surprised but quite amenable as Tessa had served Horizons well over the years, and when she'd asked that the possibility of her leaving be kept private he'd also agreed, and wondered at the same time if it had anything to do with his top man being headhunted by a Canadian hospital.

When Tessa went for the check-up early on the Friday morning of that first week, Drake was waiting. She'd had a blood test the day before in the endocrine clinic with better results than before and once he had done his examination of the offending eye he said, 'It begins to look as if I won't need to cross the Atlantic to check progress. The medication that you're on seems to be working fine'.

For a moment she felt weak with relief. But that thought was swiftly followed by the realisation that everything had its price. His next and last consultation would be her final goodbye to him, and it would be beyond bearing.

It was early September. Poppy had a place reserved at the nearest pre-school, but now it was beginning to look as if she was going to receive that part of her education elsewhere. Tessa still hadn't found a suitable place for them to live until she saw a house similar to the cottage for sale in a Devon coastal resort. It had a good pre-school nearby, and she decided to drive down there during the coming weekend to look the place over.

The idea would have been great if it hadn't been that with every mile in that direction on the Saturday her concerns regarding Poppy being separated from Lizzie's twin boys, and Randolph fretting because he wasn't going to see enough of her, were assuming gigantic proportions, and halfway there she stopped the car in a lay-by and decided to turn back.

Not because she'd changed her mind about leaving but because the place she'd been heading towards was too far away for an easy relationship to be maintained with Lizzie's boys and, of course, Poppy's beloved grandfather. How could she be so cruel as to contemplate taking his granddaughter so far away?

Yet those thoughts didn't solve the problem of leaving Horizons and Glenminster and all that they stood for to stop Drake from moving to Canada. Tessa knew that she had only herself to blame for the situation she found herself in. How had it come to this? At first she would have been delighted that he was leaving her alone—when had she changed her mind?

When she pulled up in front of the cottage the thought came that one week had already gone before

Drake flew out there and she was floundering with no idea where to go before he came back.

The phone was ringing as she put the key in the lock and on answering it she was surprised to hear her Aunt Sophie on the line once again. But when Tessa heard what she had to say it was as if someone, somewhere was looking after her.

'I did so enjoy our chat,' said the sixty-year-old keep-fit fanatic, 'even though I caused you alarm when I mentioned the thyroid connection between the women of our family. I would love to see you and Poppy and wonder if you and your little girl would like to come and stay with me for a while. I have lots of room and you'd be most welcome for as long as you'd like.'

'We'd be delighted,' Tessa said weakly.

Sophie, her mother's younger sister, lived on a part of the coast not too far away for Randolph to see his granddaughter quite often and Poppy to see the twins, yet distant enough for them to be away from Glenminster as far as Drake was concerned. If she liked it there, maybe she might see a house that would be suitable for them with a school close by, and even a hospital not too far away where she could put her training to good use.

'So when can you come?' her aunt was asking.

'Would next weekend be too soon?' she questioned.

'Not at all,' was the reply, and Tessa sank down onto the nearest chair, relieved yet tearful. Everything would work out for the best now, wouldn't it?

* * *

During the week that followed, the talk around the hospital was that Drake would be crazy not to accept the offer from a much larger and more prestigious hospital than their own, but would be sorely missed. As Tessa listened to the gossip she prayed that her departure would keep him where he belonged, enjoying life in the house that he was so set on buying, instead of having to give up the dream.

The fact that she also was involved in departure plans wasn't known generally as the chairman was keeping his word and Jennifer was too head over heels in love with the new man in her life to take much notice of what was going on anywhere else.

The more Drake thought about a move across the Atlantic the less he was looking forward to it. He'd gone to Switzerland for prestige and had got it, wrapped around with regrets over what he'd lost in the process.

It had stood to sense that in the time he'd been gone she would have found someone else to fill the gap he'd left, but nothing could have prepared him for the enchanting small child that Tessa had adopted who had all her love and devotion.

She had offered in recent days to move out of the area so that he would stay, but no way was he going to allow her to do that. He wanted her in his life now more than ever, and would be devastated if she wasn't there when he got back from Canada.

If he hadn't already agreed to attend the appointment with the Canadians he would forget the whole thing. He hadn't seen anything of her in days, and when she came for his last examination of her eye this Friday he was going to repeat what he'd said about her not leaving Glenminster.

Almost everything Tessa possessed was going to be put into storage once Drake had gone until she found the right place to live, and when she called at Randolph's on the way home on the Thursday night before her last Friday of residence in Glenminster there was a chill in the air that indicated that Poppy's grandfather was not pleased with her plans for the future.

'We aren't going to be too far away,' she told him reassuringly. 'I will bring Poppy to see you as often as I can.'

'And are you going to give me a new address where I can get in touch?' he asked crustily.

'I will when I've got one,' she promised, 'and in the meantime I've made a temporary arrangement with my Aunt Sophie and will give you her phone number.'

'So what has Drake to do with all of this?' he wanted to know.

'Everything and nothing,' was the reply, and he had to be satisfied with that.

That same morning Tessa had told Jennifer that the following day would be her last at Horizons and her secretary had gazed at her in astonishment.

'So no fanfare of trumpets at *your* departure,'

she'd said incredulously. 'I wouldn't be surprised if there's a brass band if Drake Melford decides to leave us. The general feeling is that no one wants him to go, but you can't begrudge him what has to be the opportunity of a lifetime.'

Tessa had turned away. What would everyone think if they knew she was responsible for him considering the move to Canada? She prayed that her leaving Glenminster would not be in vain. That when Drake came back and saw she was gone he would stay and be happy, and perhaps having given up on her might one day meet someone less difficult to love.

It had come, the final check-up for her eye problem with Drake, and she made her way to his consulting room with dragging steps.

What she was hoping was that he would return to the place they both loved and that, whatever decision he'd made while in Canada, he wouldn't leave Horizons once he discovered that she'd gone. She wanted him to be happy in the house of his dreams and fulfilled with the work he did at the hospital, while she would seek a return to the contentment of sorts that she'd found while they'd been apart.

Tessa looked tired, he thought when she appeared. There was a crease across her brow and a listlessness about her that indicated inward weariness. But one thing was sure, she would be relieved to see him go after the telling off he'd given her.

Yet there was no way he could let her disappear

from his life, he loved her too much. He was going to make one last attempt to show her how much he cared when he came back from Canada, and if she still didn't want him near, well, he would just persist until she did.

For one thing, his beautiful house was meant to be lived in, not used as a holiday home, and for another was the knowledge that a little girl wanted him as her daddy and he wasn't going to let her down on that.

He'd told Tessa that he was going to accept the offer from the Canadians in a moment of frustration and ever since had wished he'd kept silent.

'What time is your flight?' she asked in a polite but disinterested kind of voice. She didn't want him to call at the cottage later in the afternoon and find her in the middle of moving.

'Half past three,' he said, and with a wry smile, 'I imagine that you are just being polite with that question as the only real emotion you are feeling with regard to my departure has to be relief.'

She flashed him a tired smile. 'I thought I was here for an eye check. Is the mind-reading a freebie?'

'No, just an observation. so if you would like to open wide we will see what has been going on behind those beautiful eyes over the last week.'

Tessa could feel tears rising, and when Drake had finished the examination she said, 'Before you tell me the final results, whether they be good or not so good, I will never forget how you have been there for me with this whole unexpected eye thing.' Before he could answer she took a photograph of a happy, smiling Poppy out of her bag and, giving it to him, said, 'I thought you might like this.'

'Yes. I would indeed,' he said, as he looked down at it. 'But I would have liked one of the two of you more.'

'I'm sure you are only saying that to be polite.'

'Not necessarily,' was the reply, and cut that discussion short. 'Your results, Tessa. The eye is back to normal. Keep on taking the medication for another couple of months to be on the safe side and it should be fine. If at any time you are worried about your vision let me know immediately.'

'Are you definitely going to accept the position if they offer it to you?' she asked, choking on the words. 'I meant what I said that day on the phone.'

'Maybe you did, and maybe I won't take the job over there. What matters is that irrespective of whatever I decide to do I find you here when I come back in two weeks' time. Don't make any sacrifices on my account, Tessa. The Canadian job is already mine if I want it.'

'And you are going there because of me?' she choked.

She held out her hand to wish him goodbye, but ignoring it he looked down onto her upturned face and kissed her just once, then, releasing her, opened the door for her and closed it behind her with a decisive click.

Speechless at the finality of the moment, Tessa

went back to her office to watch for Drake's departure from the big house in time to catch his three-thirty flight.

When a taxi arrived and his baggage had been put in the boot he paused for a moment before seating himself in the back of the vehicle and glanced across to where her office was. It took all her willpower not to rush outside and beg him to stay, but thankfully it wasn't his final departure.

That, she hoped, would not come, and she prayed that when he returned Drake might forget about Canada on finding her gone and decide to stay in Glenminster where he belonged. Otherwise what she was planning to do would be a waste of both their lives.

Her furniture would be going into storage in the late afternoon and the park bench, which was covered by waterproof sheeting on the patio at the back of the cottage, was going to be transported by haulage to her aunt's home, later in the day.

All that she would have to do at the end of her last working day at the hospital would be to check that all was secure at the cottage and collect Poppy from Lizzie's house for the last time before they went to the bed and breakfast place where she had booked them in for the night.

It had been a painful farewell for the two friends, who had kept what was happening in the background from the children to avoid tears, but she was determined to make a fresh start with Poppy, and Lizzie at least understood her reasons, even if she didn't agree with the decision.

Tessa had brought a snack with her to serve as their evening meal at the bed and breakfast place and once they'd eaten she consoled a fretful Poppy, who didn't like the strange place she had brought her to with the assurance that the next day they would be at the seaside. Then she'd tucked her up in the big double bed that graced the room and, once she was sleeping, eased herself in beside her daughter and tried not to think about those last moments she'd spent with Drake in his consulting room.

After an early breakfast she stopped off at the cottage to see if the bench had been picked up yet and was relieved to see that it had. Then one of the strangest days Tessa had ever known got under way, and as the miles flashed past the enormity of what she was undertaking was beginning to register.

It was fortunate she'd managed to leave while Drake was away, she thought. She couldn't have done it with him being anywhere near, and now the die was cast and the future that not so long ago had looked contented was in front of her. She tried not to think of it as bleak—indeed, thinking of Poppy's joy at going to the seaside helped her to smile.

She had been anxious to make sure that her scooter was in the car boot before they set off, and now she was asleep after such an early start when she'd been bewildered by what was happening but excited too because they were going to be staying at the seaside and she had brought her bucket and spade on the promise of it.

Tessa had found her looking wistfully through the window at the front of the cottage a few times since the day when she'd invited Drake to lunch, but she hadn't mentioned him, except for one night when Tessa had heard her cry 'Daddy' in her sleep.

But now in the excitement of what was going on in her life he wasn't mentioned and Poppy didn't watch out for him as before.

They received a warm welcome from her aunt, who had prepared a double bedroom for the two of them, and had a lovely meal ready for the travellers at the end of a long day, and when Poppy was asleep later in the evening Sophie said gently, 'Tessa, you have the look of someone who is running away from something. Is it a man?'

'Yes,' she said. 'The love of my life left me, then he came back, and now he's leaving again. I can't cope.'

'Did he leave you for another woman?' her aunt asked.

Her smile was wry. 'No, it was his career that I had to compete with.'

'And what was that?'

'Eye surgery, ophthalmology.'

'And where is he now?'

'Debating whether to accept a position in Canada to get away from how I've been pushing him away.

I felt that if I left Glenminster he might decide to stay as he loves the place.'

'It sounds as if you care for him a lot.'

'Yes, I do. But I hurt so much when he left me that I'm afraid of it happening again, and to make matters worse Poppy is drawn to Drake like a magnet. He and I feel that she thinks he's the father that she lost in the car crash as we are told that he looks very much like him.'

'So stay here as long as you like,' Sophie said. 'Let your hurts heal by the sea and the golden sands, and, Tessa, you will know when the time is right to decide who you want to spend the rest of your life with.'

When the plane touched down in the UK Drake gave a sigh of relief. The journey had seemed to take for ever and he wanted to get back to Glenminster with all speed. He was going to ask Tessa to marry him, and if she refused he was going to keep on asking until she said yes.

The Canadian set-up had been excellent and he'd thought a few times that not so long ago he would have accepted the offer immediately, grabbed it with both hands like a precious gift. But he was no longer the same person as the one who had left Tessa with scarcely a word of goodbye and had spent the next three years wishing he hadn't.

He had bought a ring of sapphires and diamonds while he'd been in Canada, regretting all the time having told her that she was the reason why he was contemplating leaving Glenminster. It had been said in a moment of frustration. He loved the place and dreamt all the time of sharing his new house with her and Poppy.

On leaving the airport, he hired a taxi to take him straight to the cottage. It was late evening, but not so late that he would expect Tessa to have gone to bed, and he didn't want to waste a moment before being with her.

But as he turned away from paying the driver Drake saw that it was in darkness. There was a 'for sale' board on display in the front garden and his heart sank. Unconvinced, he rang the doorbell several times but got no response, and then went round to the back, only to find no signs of life there either. He thought grimly that it was going to be his turn to be left in despair and it served him right, but where to start looking for Tessa and Poppy?

Were they staying with Lizzie and Daniel? It seemed the most likely place. He checked the time. The autumn dusk was falling over the town. It wasn't fair to pressure Lizzie for Tessa's location until he was calmer, and maybe she wouldn't want to tell him where she was even then.

A better report on what had been happening while he was away might be available from Horizons tomorrow. Surely someone there would know where Tessa was, either the chairman or her secretary maybe.

He unpacked, had a shower and sat outside on the terrace of the house he had found so depressing and soulless, though it felt almost cosy after seeing Tessa's cottage dark and empty in the autumn night.

That day in his consulting room when he'd told her that if he liked the set-up in Canada he would take the job to get away from her was starkly clear in his mind and he'd never stopped regretting making the comment. Now he knew it must have pushed her too far.

CHAPTER NINE

THE NEXT MORNING he rang the chairman at home to ask if he had any knowledge of where Tessa had moved to and was told he had no idea, that the only thing he knew was that Tessa had asked him if he would allow her to skip the usual four weeks' notice.

He'd agreed reluctantly, and she'd left the same day that Drake had flown out to Canada.

'And since you're back, have you come to a decision about the job in Canada?' finished the chairman.

'I'm staying here,' Drake told him. 'I care for Horizons too much to go elsewhere.' And amidst the other man's relief he thought, and that goes for Tessa too when I find her. I care too much for her to ever want to be anywhere other than here with her. She has given up much that meant a lot to her to make me stay. But surely she knows that if she isn't with me, life will be meaningless?

After that he went to what had been Tessa's office to have a word with her secretary and saw that a temporary replacement was already sitting behind

her desk, which added another ominous note to his
enquiries, and when Jennifer said that she hadn't
known that Tessa was leaving until the very last
moment and had no idea where she was planning
to move to he gave up on that one.

He could no longer ignore the fact that Lizzie and
Daniel were the only people who would know where
she was, and he hoped he could persuade them to
tell him. He'd had an exhausting day, bringing his
appointments up to date and taking the clinic that
his staff had been in charge of during his absence,
but like the cottage of the night before there was no
answer when he rang the doorbell. Luckily, a neighbour told him they were on holiday. So using the
moment to ask a question he said, 'Have Lizzie's
friend and her little girl gone with them?'

'No, just the four of them—Lizzie, Daniel and
the children,' he was told.

So much for that, Drake thought grimly, pointing the car back towards Horizons. As he was driving past the park his eyes widened: the bench had
gone! All the benches had gone, and been replaced
by new ones. Was it a sign, telling him that it really
was over between the two of them? He wouldn't take
no for an answer this time, he was going to find her
and tell her how he felt. He should have done it ages
ago, but somehow his pride and her prickliness had
got in the way. This time would be different.

After his unsuccessful visit to Lizzie's house
Drake rang Randolph, who told him that he didn't
know where Tessa and Poppy were, but she had

promised to be in touch the moment they were set-tled somewhere new, and that was it.

'What is it with the two of you?' he asked. 'Any-one can see that you are meant to be together.'

'Not quite everyone,' Drake told him. 'Tessa doesn't, and I'm to blame for that.'

The old man sighed. 'So work your magic on her. We both want her back here, don't we?'

'Yes, we do,' he told him flatly. 'I'm doing my best. I'll find her.'

They were having a picnic on the beach, Tessa and Poppy with Lizzie and her family, who had just ar-rived in the area for a short holiday further along the coast so as not to draw attention to Sophie's house guests, though it was unlikely that anyone from Glenminster would be visiting the isolated coastal village.

Her aunt had gone to a keep-fit class in the vil-lage hall, and the children were splashing in the shallows after making a sandcastle.

But the adults were having a serious talk as Lizzie reported that Drake was apparently back from Canada and hadn't been tempted by what was on offer there, from the looks of it. She had rung the hospital in the guise of a prospective patient and been told that Dr Melford was back and was taking appointments as he would be staying on the staff of Horizons for the foreseeable future.

'So Drake is back where he belongs,' Tessa said. But the relief at his decision to stay was complicated by not knowing how she was going to endure a future that was grey and empty, like that of an exile from a promised land, and as if Lizzie had read her mind she had a question to ask.

'So are you going to go back there now you're sure that he isn't leaving?'

Tessa shook her head. 'No, not unless I'm asked.' And for the rest of the afternoon she picnicked and played with the children until the light began to fade, then Lizzie and her family, who were leaving the next morning to travel further along the coast for another few days, said their goodbyes with a promise to see her again soon.

Almost a week had gone by and it was as if Tessa had disappeared off the face of the earth, Drake thought. No one at the hospital had seen her or knew of her whereabouts. There was no sign of Lizzie and Daniel having returned from their holiday, but he would try again tonight, he vowed, and if they were still away he would ask the obliging neighbour if she'd had any messages from them that might point him towards locating Tessa.

The house had the same look of being unoccupied as on the other occasion when he'd called, but this time he rang next door's bell and the same woman as before appeared.

'I've been looking out for you,' she said. 'They'll be back tomorrow. I got a card a couple of days ago. It seems they've been staying at a place called Bretton Sands.'

'Fine!' he said. 'I'll call round tomorrow night and surprise them.' And went on his way thinking that he'd heard the name before, but it didn't sound like somewhere Tessa would make a beeline for. The kind neighbour had also said the first time he'd called that Tessa and Poppy weren't with them, so he was still none the wiser.

It was in the middle of the night that he awoke wide-eyed and raised himself up off the pillows. At the time of Tessa's aunt phoning and mentioning that the women of their family were prone to thyroid issues he had recalled that she was the one that Tessa had once told him lived in a remote village miles down the coast. Was it possible that was where she'd gone?

There was no way he could set off now to find out. A full day in Theatre and on the wards was ahead of him, but he could set off the moment he'd finished, and if he found himself to be mistaken he could drive all night and get back in time for the next day's duties.

If Tessa was to be found in the place that he was heading for, someone else would have to take his appointments until he came back down to earth… And there was the ring. If he took it with him it might bring him his heart's desire, the woman he loved as his beautiful bride.

The day that followed seemed never-ending but Drake's attention to his patients was faultless. Blindness was everyone's terror and if it was possible to prevent it, he had the skills to help.

His last case of the day was a middle-aged woman brought in as an emergency with an eye injured from the cork of a bottle of home-made wine flying off explosively when she'd been trying to open it, and was in a state of shock.

This time he decided to let his second in command take over while he watched, and while he inspected the eye with the ophthalmoscope Drake listened to his comments, and then took over to see if he agreed with his findings that the blow from the cork had been prevented from doing serious damage by the eyelid's reflex action, and that the bruising and soreness would disappear in a few days.

It seemed that his findings were correct and he said, 'Well done!' and left him to give the good news to the anxious patient.

As soon as he had been home to change Drake set off to find what he now knew was real love, the kind that Tessa had wanted, the kind that was ready to give rather than take, and prayed that he'd find her at the place off the beaten track called Bretton Sands.

Poppy was asleep, sun-kissed and wind-blown after all the fun she'd had with her friends on the beach, and as Tessa moved restlessly from room to room, with Lizzie's news uppermost in her mind, her aunt said, 'There's a full moon and the tide is out. Why don't you go for a stroll along the sands while I keep an eye on Poppy?' and because of all things she needed quiet and the time to think, she followed the suggestion.

Outside it was warm, with moonlight turning the sea to silver, and when Tessa left the sand behind and came to rocks she perched herself on the first one she arrived at and sat silhouetted against the night sky.

Drake had parked the car and was moving along the short promenade, seeking someone to ask where he might find Tessa's Aunt Sophie. He wasn't sure of her surname, which would make the questioning tricky. Even trickier was the fact that there was no one to ask, the place being deserted.

As he approached the end of the paved area and was about to turn back he saw her, seated on a rock, gazing out to sea. He said her name softly, and the wind must have carried it out towards her for it could not have been loud enough for her to hear.

Tessa turned, startled, and as their glances held she exclaimed, 'Drake! How did you know where to find me? No one knows I'm here except Aunt Sophie, Lizzie and her family...and Randolph.'

He was smiling. 'I'd tried everywhere else and no one knew where you'd gone, until on a second visit to Lizzie and Daniel's place yesterday their neighbour said she'd had a card from a place called Bretton Sands, which didn't ring a bell at first. But in the middle of last night it dawned on me that your Aunt Sophie lived somewhere along that coast, and as soon as I'd finished for the day I was on my way, praying that I hadn't got it wrong.'

'Why did you change your mind about leaving Horizons?' she asked softly from her perch on the rock.

'Because I love you, and know that you love me, or you wouldn't have left Glenminster for my sake.' He produced the ring and said, 'I bought this while I was in Canada. Will you let me put it on your finger and in the near future place a wedding ring next to it? Will you marry me, Tessa?'

'Yes,' she said, finding her voice, and when she stretched her arm across the divide that separated them he put it on her finger. Looking down at the sapphires and diamonds, she said, 'It's beautiful, Drake. I shall feel truly blessed wearing it. The only way I knew to show you how much I loved you was by moving out of Glenminster to give you a reason for staying.'

'Yes, I know,' he said softly, 'but you overlooked one thing. I can't live without you.'

He opened his arms and took her hands in his and as she stepped down from the rock and was safe inside his hold he said laughingly, 'What do you think Poppy will say when she hears about this?'

'It goes without saying, she'll be delighted,' she told him, and then he kissed her and at last life was how she had longed for it to be.

CHAPTER TEN

THEY HAD TO sort out where Tessa and Poppy were going to sleep when they arrived back in Glenminster the following day. Drake had spent the night in Bretton Sands' only hotel and had been greeted rapturously by Poppy the next morning.

There was no way they could sleep at the cottage as even the bedding had gone into storage, but there was one thing that hadn't, and it had been an emotional moment when he'd seen the park bench on Aunt Sophie's patio.

'Where on earth has that come from?' he'd asked huskily.

'I was driving past when the workmen were taking them away and I bought it from them as I had to have something to remember you by,' she'd told him.

'What a lovely surprise,' he'd said, holding her close, 'and when we get back I have a surprise for you.' Turning to her aunt, who had been beaming at them in her delight at seeing her niece so happy, 'You must come and stay with us, Aunt Sophie,

when we are settled. I'm indebted to you for looking after my precious ones.'

And now Drake was inside the hospital, rearranging
his appointments so that he could take a couple of
days off while they arranged their wedding. It was,
of course, going to take place in the gardens of the
hotel where he'd taken Tessa for lunch that day, and
she was making up the other four-poster bed in the
big house so that she and Poppy would have somewhere to sleep until the night of the wedding.

When he came in and saw what she was doing
Drake said, 'For once this place won't seem so cheer-
less tonight, we might not even notice the creaking.
Are you ready for the scenic tour?'

She smiled across at him. 'Of course. Is it the
surprise that you promised?'

'It is indeed because I don't want you to get any
wrong ideas that I might be expecting you to live
in this place.'

He couldn't wait to take her and Poppy to see his
new home, and was hoping that they would love it
as much as he did. Tessa would adore the idea of
planning the furnishing of its empty rooms in the
short time they had before the wedding, and the
large garden was just crying out for some children's
swings and slides.

When they arrived at the village that Horizons
had chosen for its yearly picnic that day, Tessa recalled how Drake had been quick to pass Poppy back
into her care after minding her and had strolled off

casually towards a house that was for sale in the last stages of construction.

She'd thought nothing of it at the time, but now here he was, turning the key in the lock, sweeping her up into his arms and carrying her over its threshold, and as she looked around her it was easy to tell why he loved the place.

It was light and airy, with clean lines, spacious rooms and fabulous views from the windows. All it needed now was to be furnished, for them to put the finishing touches to it that were their choice. As Poppy gazed around her in wonderment he said gently, 'This is where we are going to live. Do you like it?''

'Yes!' she cried. 'Can the boys come to play?'

'Of course they can. We are all going to have a lovely time living here, aren't we, Mummy?' he asked Tessa.

She nodded, and told the man who had once held her heart in careless hands, and had come back to give *his* into *her* keeping, 'Yes. We are. It will be wonderful beyond words.'

'We have such a lot of time to make up for, Tessa,' he said softly. 'Does that make you glad or sorry?'

'Just so glad,' she whispered. 'Happy that we are together at last.'

Lizzie and Poppy were the bridesmaids on the day of the wedding with Randolph giving the bride away and the chairman in the role of Drake's best man, while the vicar from the local church was to marry them.

It was autumn and the day had dawned with fruit ripening on the trees and everywhere to be seen were the bronzes and golds of the season.

The wedding wasn't a big family affair as neither bride nor groom had many relatives, their parents having been lost to them at different times over the years, but plenty of staff from Horizons who weren't on duty were there to offer their best wishes.

Tessa's white wedding dress had lily of the valley looped along the hemline and she was carrying a bouquet of the palest of pink roses. As Drake, standing beneath an archway of the same kind of flowers, watched her walking slowly towards him along the main walkway of the hotel gardens, he recognised them.

Lily of the valley and pink roses had been the flowers in the corsage he had given her that night on the river boat when she'd fastened it to her suit and asked him to dance, and the thought brought even more joy to a day that was already overflowing with it.

The marriage had taken place. The gold band of matrimony was in place next to the beautiful sapphire and diamond ring. The festivities were over and Poppy was asleep in the back of the car after all the day's excitement. But when they arrived at the house, she opened her eyes as Drake carried her upstairs and said, 'Can I sleep in my bridesmaid's dress, Daddy?'

'I don't see why not,' he said, and when he'd laid her gently against the pillows they watched her eyelids droop, and before they'd got to the door she was asleep again.

It was late afternoon and a September sun would soon be setting on their special day. As they strolled around the garden of their new home, with the park bench safely inside a flower-decked arbour, Drake said with laughing tenderness, 'How long do you think we should wait before we give Poppy a brother or a sister?'

'No time at all,' Tessa suggested laughingly, and she could tell that he thought it was a good idea.

EPILOGUE

THEY HAD MADE love with the evening sun laying strands of gold across them while Poppy slept in dreamland. It had been as good as it had always been, wild, sweet and passionate.

But instead of it being the end for them, it was only the beginning of lives that would be built on the rock of their love for each other, instead of the shifting sands of desire and a need for acclaim.

* * * * *

MILLS & BOON®
Hardback – March 2015

ROMANCE

The Taming of Xander Sterne	Carole Mortimer
In the Brazilian's Debt	Susan Stephens
At the Count's Bidding	Caitlin Crews
The Sheikh's Sinful Seduction	Dani Collins
The Real Romero	Cathy Williams
His Defiant Desert Queen	Jane Porter
Prince Nadir's Secret Heir	Michelle Conder
Princess's Secret Baby	Carol Marinelli
The Renegade Billionaire	Rebecca Winters
The Playboy of Rome	Jennifer Faye
Reunited with Her Italian Ex	Lucy Gordon
Her Knight in the Outback	Nikki Logan
Baby Twins to Bind Them	Carol Marinelli
The Firefighter to Heal Her Heart	Annie O'Neil
Thirty Days to Win His Wife	Andrea Laurence
Her Forbidden Cowboy	Charlene Sands
The Blackstone Heir	Dani Wade
After Hours with Her Ex	Maureen Child

MEDICAL

Tortured by Her Touch	Dianne Drake
It Happened in Vegas	Amy Ruttan
The Family She Needs	Sue MacKay
A Father for Poppy	Abigail Gordon

MILLS & BOON®
Large Print – March 2015

ROMANCE

A Virgin for His Prize	Lucy Monroe
The Valquez Seduction	Melanie Milburne
Protecting the Desert Princess	Carol Marinelli
One Night with Morelli	Kim Lawrence
To Defy a Sheikh	Maisey Yates
The Russian's Acquisition	Dani Collins
The True King of Dahaar	Tara Pammi
The Twelve Dates of Christmas	Susan Meier
At the Chateau for Christmas	Rebecca Winters
A Very Special Holiday Gift	Barbara Hannay
A New Year Marriage Proposal	Kate Hardy

HISTORICAL

Darian Hunter: Duke of Desire	Carole Mortimer
Rescued by the Viscount	Anne Herries
The Rake's Bargain	Lucy Ashford
Unlaced by Candlelight	Various
The Warrior's Winter Bride	Denise Lynn

MEDICAL

A Secret Shared...	Marion Lennox
Flirting with the Doc of Her Dreams	Janice Lynn
The Doctor Who Made Her Love Again	Susan Carlisle
The Maverick Who Ruled Her Heart	Susan Carlisle
After One Forbidden Night...	Amber McKenzie
Dr Perfect on Her Doorstep	Lucy Clark

MILLS & BOON®
Hardback – April 2015

ROMANCE

The Billionaire's Bridal Bargain	Lynne Graham
At the Brazilian's Command	Susan Stephens
Carrying the Greek's Heir	Sharon Kendrick
The Sheikh's Princess Bride	Annie West
His Diamond of Convenience	Maisey Yates
Olivero's Outrageous Proposal	Kate Walker
The Italian's Deal for I Do	Jennifer Hayward
Virgin's Sweet Rebellion	Kate Hewitt
The Millionaire and the Maid	Michelle Douglas
Expecting the Earl's Baby	Jessica Gilmore
Best Man for the Bridesmaid	Jennifer Faye
It Started at a Wedding...	Kate Hardy
Just One Night?	Carol Marinelli
Meant-To-Be Family	Marion Lennox
The Soldier She Could Never Forget	Tina Beckett
The Doctor's Redemption	Susan Carlisle
Wanted: Parents for a Baby!	Laura Iding
His Perfect Bride?	Louisa Heaton
Twins on the Way	Janice Maynard
The Nanny Plan	Sarah M. Anderson

MILLS & BOON®
Large Print – April 2015

ROMANCE

Taken Over by the Billionaire	Miranda Lee
Christmas in Da Conti's Bed	Sharon Kendrick
His for Revenge	Caitlin Crews
A Rule Worth Breaking	Maggie Cox
What The Greek Wants Most	Maya Blake
The Magnate's Manifesto	Jennifer Hayward
To Claim His Heir by Christmas	Victoria Parker
Snowbound Surprise for the Billionaire	Michelle Douglas
Christmas Where They Belong	Marion Lennox
Meet Me Under the Mistletoe	Cara Colter
A Diamond in Her Stocking	Kandy Shepherd

HISTORICAL

Strangers at the Altar	Marguerite Kaye
Captured Countess	Ann Lethbridge
The Marquis's Awakening	Elizabeth Beacon
Innocent's Champion	Meriel Fuller
A Captain and a Rogue	Liz Tyner

MEDICAL

It Started with No Strings...	Kate Hardy
One More Night with Her Desert Prince...	Jennifer Taylor
Flirting with Dr Off-Limits	Robin Gianna
From Fling to Forever	Avril Tremayne
Dare She Date Again?	Amy Ruttan
The Surgeon's Christmas Wish	Annie O'Neil

MILLS & BOON®

Why shop at millsandboon.co.uk?

Each year, thousands of romance readers find their perfect read at millsandboon.co.uk. That's because we're passionate about bringing you the very best romantic fiction. Here are some of the advantages of shopping at www.millsandboon.co.uk:

* **Get new books first**—you'll be able to buy your favourite books one month before they hit the shops

* **Get exclusive discounts**—you'll also be able to buy our specially created monthly collections, with up to 50% off the RRP

* **Find your favourite authors**—latest news, interviews and new releases for all your favourite authors and series on our website, plus ideas for what to try next

* **Join in**—once you've bought your favourite books, don't forget to register with us to rate, review and join in the discussions

Visit **www.millsandboon.co.uk**
for all this and more today!